Once Upon a Gothic

by

Alicia Dean

Once Upon a Gothic

COPYRIGHT © 2021 by Alicia Dean

Cover Art by *The Wild Rose Press, Inc.*

The Wild Rose Press, Inc.
PO Box 708
Adams Basin, NY 14410-0708
Visit us at www.thewildrosepress.com

Publishing History
First Edition, 2021
Trade Paperback ISBN 978-1-5092-3681-7
Digital ISBN 978-1-5092-3682-4

Published in the United States of America

LADY IN THE MIST...

A scream left my throat. I couldn't think straight. Terror sent blood rushing through my eardrums, and it was several moments before I recognized Clinton's voice. "Lillian? Are you all right?"

On shaking legs, I rushed to the door, mindless of the dark. I jerked it open and summoned all my willpower not to launch into Clinton's arms. In the faint glow of the flashlight he held, I could barely make out his silhouette, but just having another human in the vicinity eased my terror.

"The power's out," I said stupidly.

~*~

HAUNTING AT SPOOK LIGHT INN...

"You *tried* to get in?" He stalked over until he stood directly in front of me, looming like a dark, angry cloud. "The carriage house is off limits. Stay away from it, do you understand me?"

I swallowed. "I wasn't going to hurt anything. I was just curio—"

"I said stay away." His voice was deadly, his eyes molten steel. "Do I make myself clear?"

For one brief moment, the fury in his eyes made me think he *might* be capable of murder after all. Namely, mine. I couldn't speak, so I only nodded. He held my gaze for a few more gut wrenching moments, then stormed away.

Praise for...

Lady in the Mist

In only a few pages, Alicia Dean delivers a well-written, strong whodunnit, mixed with a viable, complex romance. Between the empowered voice of her narrator, Lily Jackson, and the enigmatic Breckenridge brothers, the characters are enthralling and relatable.

~ *Author Fierce Dolan*

~*~

Shades of Victoria Holt. Spooky atmosphere from the get-go. I didn't want to put it down.

~ *Author Diane Burton*

Haunting at Spook Light Inn:

Haunting at Spook Light Inn by Alicia Dean has the creepy, edge-of-your-seat suspense and genuine, relatable characters I've come to expect from this author. Being a native Oklahoman, I found the tale of the ominous Quapaw Spook Light especially fascinating and hope to go and check it out for myself soon.

~ *Author Anna Kittrell*

~*~

This book reminded me of all the old Gothics I used to love back in the day. From the tone to the setting to the characters and plot, this author has the genre down to a science. While the story takes place in modern day, she could very well have changed their clothing and transportation and transported us back in time. Very well done. Move over Victoria Holt!

~ *Author Jannine Gallant*

Dedication

To my sister, Ruth. Since our days of playing Barbie's together as children, you've encouraged my flights of fantasy. Thank you for your years of love and support.

And for all lovers of the classic gothic mysteries by authors such as Victoria Holt, Daphne du Maurier, Barbara Michaels, Phyllis A. Whitney, and many more. I read them growing up and have never forgotten them. I'm pleased to help bring the genre back into the modern world.

Lady in the Mist

Chapter One

My first glimpse of Breckenridge Manor sent a trickle of fear down my spine. The gloomy afternoon sky shadowed the house's soulless windows. Haze-shrouded spires extended upward as if desperately trying to escape the bonds of the stony cliff. I tightened my grip on the ferry rail.

"Intimidating isn't it?"

Turning, I found a man standing at my elbow. He looked to be around thirty—three years or so older than me—and would have been nice-looking had it not been for the hard glint in his blue eyes and the bitter twist to his mouth. His goatee was the same shade as sandy-blond hair that brushed the collar of his brown suede jacket.

"Yes, a little." I looked back at the house. Purple and gold mist swirled around the bottom of the foundation, the structure seeming to rise from the water like some mystical sea creature.

"Breckenridge Manor is an evil place."

I turned in surprise at the vehemence in his tone. "How can a house be evil?"

His mouth twisted further into bitterness. "Not the house, exactly, more like the owners."

The owners. My prospective future employers. The blast of the ferry horn prevented further speech. When it ended, he said, "Where are you from?"

"Cincinnati."

"That's a long way from Maine. What brings you to Shoal Harbor?"

"A job. I don't have it yet, but I'm keeping my fingers crossed."

"Hmmm. Not a lot of job openings on the island. Let me guess. You're the new nanny for Andrew Breckenridge."

I smiled. "I wouldn't exactly call the position a *nanny*. Andrew is older than I am."

His returning smile held no humor. "Trust me, you'll be playing nanny. You obviously haven't met—" He halted as the chilly November breeze picked up, bringing with it the fresh scent of salt water. His eyes narrowed. "Listen," he whispered.

I did, straining my ears, although not knowing what I was listening for. At first, all I heard was the sigh of the wind, the distant cry of a seagull, the water lapping against the ferry's hull. Then, another sound reached my ears. A shiver raced over my skin when I heard a low, sorrowful moan. Although I knew it had to be the wind, it sounded eerily like a woman's cry.

I met my companion's gaze, and he smiled with satisfaction.

"You heard it, didn't you?"

I swallowed back a tremor of unease. "What was it?"

A satisfied smirk touched his mouth. "Legend has it that it's the cry of the Breckenridge women. Those who've died tragic deaths."

"Ghosts?" I tried to scoff, but it came out a nervous laugh. "That's just silly."

"Is it? There's a lot you don't know about your prospective employers." He shoved his hands in his

2

pants pockets and leaned a hip against the rail, looking out over the dark blue water.

"Like what?"

He shrugged. "You'll learn soon enough. If you have any sense of self-preservation, you'll climb back on the next ferry out and never return."

I wanted to mock the over-the-top creepy vibe he was putting out, but the finger of dread traveling over my spine prevented me from doing so. "I want this job. Besides, I don't scare easily."

He studied me intently. "Maybe you'll make out okay. You're not really their type. Blue eyes—check. Fair skin—check. But the Breckenridge men normally go for tall, leggy, big-busted blondes."

I ran a hand over my dark hair self-consciously. He said it like I was entering the lair of some kind of monstrous beasts. Before I could decide what to make of his odd and somewhat intimidating behavior, we arrived at the dock where perhaps a dozen people waited.

One person in particular stood out, a guy about my age. Even though I couldn't clearly make out his features from this distance, I had the impression that he was attractive.

The ferry drew closer. He caught me staring and grinned. From behind his back, he pulled out a sign, holding it above his head. I squinted, peering at the large bold letters that spelled out *Lillian?*

Definitely here for me. Was he one of the Breckenridge brothers? He appeared too young to be Clinton Breckenridge and, considering Andrew's mental instability, it was highly unlikely he would come to pick me up.

The ferry captain—an older gentleman with gray whiskers and a paunch peeking between the buttons of his jacket—unlatched and opened the gate, bidding goodbye to his passengers. He'd explained during the ride about how Shoal Harbor's shopping, fishing and beaches made it a popular tourist attraction. He didn't have to sell me on the place, I had to be there whether I wanted to or not.

I disembarked, drawing closer to the guy with the sign.

When I was six feet from him, my suspicions were confirmed. The guy was more than just attractive. He was the most beautiful man I'd ever seen. He had tousled dark blond hair, thick black eyelashes framing glorious blue-green eyes, and muscled forearms tapering down to black leather bands on each wrist. Dimples slanted either side of his lips when he flashed me a smile that revealed perfect white teeth.

I reached him, and he released one of the hands holding the sign. Taking my fingers in his, he lightly shook my hand.

"Lillian Jackson?"

"Yes." I tugged my hand from his grip.

"Nice to meet you. I'm Drew Breckenridge."

Drew Breckenridge? My earlier assumption was incorrect. My potential patient *had* been sent to pick me up. Perhaps he was more stable than I'd been led to believe.

****

Drew stowed my luggage in the trunk of a sleek black Aston Martin, then opened the passenger door, waiting as I slid inside before climbing into the driver's seat and smoothly gunning the engine. Settling back into the plush upholstery, I nearly purred. The soft leather cocooned me like a cozy, warm cloud.

"You have a gorgeous car," I told him.

"My *brother* has a gorgeous car but thank you. It belonged to our father."

I knew from speaking with the job service that referred me that both parents had died. Their mother's death was fairly recent, but their father had been dead for fifteen years. So, in spite of its pristine condition, the car wasn't new.

We drove along winding roads, the sea on one side—so close, we seemed to be cruising on its glittering surface—towering pine trees on the other. I stared out the window, awed by the scenery. A cluster of small boats bobbed on crystal blue water framed by jagged cliffs. So beautiful here. So Old World. Brooklyn, my best friend, would love it. I remembered I hadn't called her to let her know I'd arrived. We'd known one another since the third grade and were roommates at the University of Cincinnati. Not having her around would be strange and foreign.

"I hope you don't mind," I said. "But I need to make a quick call. I promised my friend I'd call when I got here."

"Good luck with that. Once you're outside town, cell service is pretty much zip."

My mouth dropped open. "No cell service? You're kidding, right?"

"'Fraid not. You can use the landline when we get to the house."

Landline?

"You have a computer, don't you?"

He chuckled and shook his head. "You're in a

whole new world now. No computers at the house."

"How do you survive?"

The smile faded, and his expression darkened. "One day at a time, sweetheart. One day at a time."

I fell silent, going back to staring out the window. This time, instead of the beautiful scenery, I saw a barren land with no means of communication. How was that even possible in this day and age?

"So, was Sebastian regaling you with dire warnings about getting mixed up with the infamous Breckenridge family?"

I forced my attention back to Drew. "Sebastian?"

"Sebastian Myers. He owns the Seafarer's Tavern in town. You were speaking with him on the ferry. He's not exactly a fan of the family."

I realized then that the man hadn't even introduced himself. As Drew guessed, he'd launched immediately into his negative opinion of the Breckenridges.

"He was just being—friendly. Welcoming me to town."

"Right." Drew snorted.

Fortunately, he didn't say more on the subject. I wasn't about to reveal what Sebastian Myers had said, and I felt uncomfortable lying.

"How was your trip?" He asked.

"It was awesome. I've never been on a ferryboat. Although I was afraid I might get seasick, the trip was actually quite pleasant, calming."

"The sea can be that way. She can also be a raging bitch." His tone was tinged with inexplicable bitterness.

"Luckily, we didn't run into any storms." I shuddered. Storms on land were terrifying enough. I couldn't imagine experiencing one on the water.

He glanced at me, his lips quirking. "So, what makes a pretty girl like you want to come to such an isolated place to care for a psychotic mental patient?"

The question took me by surprise. He was mocking himself, yet he couldn't be thrilled at the prospect of his brother hiring a "nanny"—to use Sebastian's word—for him.

"I had to leave school, so I needed to find work. There wasn't much left for me in Cincinnati after my father's—" I blinked back tears. "My father's death. I saw the ad and…well…here I am."

"Yes, here you are."

The sarcastic amusement in his tone increased my discomfort. "Is there something I should know?" I'd hoped my words would come out firm, confident, but instead, they sounded unsteady and ill at ease.

"Just be prepared when you meet my brother. Stay on your toes, and you might sufficiently pass muster so that he'll actually hire you."

"You don't think he'll like me?"

"He doesn't like anyone. Especially women. He *enjoys* them. He just doesn't like them." He took his eyes off the road and ran his gaze over me. "What's important is not letting him know how much *I* like you."

I shifted uncomfortably, tugging the hem of my skirt down over my knees. I wore a silk pearl-white blouse and black pencil skirt, wanting to make a good first impression in the interview, but now I felt exposed. And concerned at the thought that Clinton Breckenridge might not hire me.

"You don't appear to be bothered that your brother feels you need a caretaker," I said.

Drew's mouth twisted into an acidic smile. "It's the lesser of two evils. If I don't have someone watching over me, he'll put me back in the institution."

Clinton Breckenridge would go so far as to lock away his younger brother? Although Drew had been diagnosed as bipolar, he seemed to be doing well. He was charming and intelligent. How could his brother feel he should be hospitalized?

I'd learned from speaking with the housekeeper on the phone that Drew was currently on a new medication, and they weren't confident that it would work. Clinton Breckenridge wanted someone with a background in psychology to keep an eye on him until it could be determined if the medication was working. From what I'd seen so far, it was working well. Admittedly, I wasn't a trained psychiatrist. However, I was less than a year away from earning my PHD when I'd been forced to leave school, and I knew enough about mental instability to know that Drew was not a candidate for institutionalization.

Silence settled between us for the remainder of the drive. After a few more minutes, Drew turned in between wrought iron gates that slowly eased back.

The drive circled around a stone fountain that rested on a perfectly sculpted lawn. Up close, the house wasn't nearly as formidable as it seemed from a distance. Although the structure was enormous, the faded red wood and the chipped paint on forest green awnings made it appear more sad than luxurious.

A man stepped off the porch and strode toward Drew's side of the car.

"My brother," Drew whispered. "And he's pissed."

Chapter Two

Drew and I both climbed out, although I did so much more reluctantly.

"What the hell do you think you're doing?" Clinton Breckenridge demanded. He looked to be perhaps five years older than Drew. He resembled his brother in the tall, muscular body type and strong-jawed facial features, but the similarities ended there. Drew's coloring was light, his manner carefree. The elder Breckenridge had darker hair, and his menacing posture gave off anything but a carefree vibe.

Drew shrugged. "I went to pick up Lillian."

"You know you're not supposed to—" Halting abruptly, Clinton glared at me over the hood of the car as if this were somehow my fault. A glint of irritation shimmered in narrowed hazel eyes. The dark stubble of facial hair didn't conceal the angry tick in his jaw.

I returned his stare and lifted my chin, not speaking. He focused his attention back on his brother.

"We'll talk about this later," he barked.

Drew tossed the keys at him and slammed the door, stalking around him to climb the steps. Clinton Breckenridge came to my side of the car where I still stood, unsure of what my next move should be, wondering how badly I needed this job. The truth was—pretty badly.

"I apologize for the display you just witnessed." He

frowned. "You're Lillian Jackson?"

"Yes." I stuck my hand out. "Nice to meet you."

He stared down at my hand for a moment as if considering ignoring it. Finally, he took it, the warmth of his fingers in contrast to the coldness of his demeanor. "Clinton Breckenridge." He quickly released me.

Drew had disappeared inside, and an older lady I presumed to be the housekeeper I'd spoken with on the phone stepped out to join us.

Faint hints of gray shone in short blonde hair and a welcoming smile spread over her unlined face. "Hello, dear. I'm Joanne Lambert. Let's go inside like civilized people. This is no way to welcome a guest." She turned a disapproving look on Clinton. I was surprised to see a trace of red color his face.

Reaching into the trunk, he retrieved my suitcase and carryon. "Is this all you have?"

"That's it." Why did I have the feeling the remark meant he found me lacking?

Once inside the house, I glimpsed a large, tastefully furnished living room just off the foyer.

"Let me show you to your room," Joanne said. "Then, you can meet with Mr. Breckenridge in the study."

"Joanne," Clinton said. "Let's not get ahead of ourselves. I'll leave her things here, and once we've completed the final interview, we'll decide if she's staying. If so, you can show her to her room."

My cheeks heated. I felt like a specimen being scrutinized by a disappointed scientist.

Joanne pulled her shoulders back. "The least you can do is allow the poor girl to freshen up. For goodness sake, where are your manners? I thought I taught you better than that."

I watched in fascination as this slight, non-threatening woman scolded the intimidating master of Breckenridge Manor.

He hesitated only slightly before giving a curt nod. "Of course. My apologies." He headed up the stairs, my overnight bag in one hand, my suitcase in the other. Joanne and I followed until he stopped in front of a door. Shouldering it open, he placed the luggage on the floor. "I'll be in the study when she's ready."

Joanne led me inside the spacious bedroom. "How was your trip?"

I smiled. "It was nice. The ferry ride was breathtaking. This is a beautiful place."

"Indeed it is. Freshen up if you'd like, rest a bit. Dinner is in two hours."

"Judging by Mr. Breckenridge's attitude, it's unlikely I'll be here at dinner time." Drew's prediction had been correct. His brother didn't like me.

"Pay no attention to him. He's a bit gruff on the outside, but he's a good man. Young Andrew raised his ire and Clinton has a problem with self-control. He shouldn't have displayed his irritation with his brother in front of you. It's unlikely he'll apologize, so I'll apologize for him."

"No apology necessary. I understand." I didn't. Not really, but I thought it the polite thing to say.

"I'll leave you now. Let me know if you need anything."

I nodded my thanks and moved farther into the room. A large, canopied bed with intricately carved wooden posts was the centerpiece. I smoothed my hand over the rich mauve coverlet with gold threads that sparkled from the reflection of the chandelier. While obviously expensive, the furnishings were worn. Like the car, the Breckenridge home and its contents were not brand new. Moving across the plush carpet to the window, I pulled the draperies back, delighted to find they opened out onto a balcony that overlooked the water. A weathered lighthouse towered above the shoreline. A flock of birds circled the spire, casting eerie shadows on the roof.

Resisting the desire to step out onto the terrace and take in the view, I retrieved my toiletry bag from my luggage and went into the bathroom where I discovered marble countertops, a marble sink with gold fixtures, and mauve and cream colored towels that were so luxurious I was hesitant to use them.

I washed my face and hands, then reapplied my make-up. I replaced my cosmetic bag and pulled out a black, velvet-encased bundle. I removed the cloth, and wistful tears pricked my eyelids. The music box had been a gift from my father to my mother on their tenth anniversary. A crystal heart rimmed in 14-karat gold sat atop the red acrylic casing. I twisted the key and strains of "Can't Help Falling in Love" filled the silence—the song my parents danced to at their wedding. My heart ached. I could still see the rapture on my mother's face when she'd opened the gift.

Other than my personal belongings, this was the only item I'd taken when I was banished from my family home. It didn't technically belong to me, but there was no way I would leave something so precious with that witch my father had married.

My stepmother had preyed upon my father's

weakness during his fight against cancer. He was heavily medicated and probably wasn't thinking clearly. I didn't know until after his death that she'd convinced him to leave everything to her. She'd immediately cut me off. The woman despised me, because I'd seen right through her the moment my father introduced us. She wasn't much older than me, and I instantly pegged her for the greedy she-devil she proved herself to be. In the end, though, she'd won. I'd lost my father and my home.

I gently wrapped the box and placed it back in my overnight bag. I couldn't continue to linger. Drawing in a deep, fortifying breath, I pushed aside my dread and went in search of Mr. Breckenridge.

****

Joanne met me at the bottom of the staircase. "Ready?" She asked. At my nod, she said, "Right this way."

I followed her down a long hallway where portraits lined the walls. We moved so quickly, I didn't have time to study them, but I assumed the various men and women were Breckenridge ancestors. I saw no photos of Drew or his brother.

Joanne and I halted in front of a closed door where Andrew's voice filtered to us. "I like her," he said with a touch of petulance.

"You don't have the final say. It seems when you like women too much, the results are less than favorable."

Drew spoke again, his voice seething with anger bordering on rage. "You have a hell of a lot of nerve bringing her up."

After a pause, Clinton Breckenridge said, "I'm

sorry." His voice softened. "Listen, I'll talk to her. I'll make the final decision, but I will take your wishes into consideration."

I met Joanne's gaze. Lips tight with disapproval, she rapped on the wood.

The door flung open and Drew appeared, shooting me a forced smile before he stalked down the hallway.

Clinton stood behind a large oak desk, his features drawn into a scowl.

"Thank you, Joanne," he said.

The housekeeper nodded. "Let me know if you'll be needing refreshments."

She left, pulling the door shut behind her. Leaving me on my own with a man whose very presence seemed to suck all the oxygen from the room.

"Come in." He motioned impatiently to a chair adjacent to his desk. "Have a seat."

I obeyed, noting as I sank into the supple cushion that the man must have an affinity for leather.

Settling into a large black chair behind his desk—leather, I presumed—he said abruptly, "I know Joanne interviewed you over the phone. She explained Andrew's issues and why we need someone to keep a careful eye on him. And that it's a temporary position? Just until we determine whether or not Drew's medication will work for him. Until he stabilizes."

I didn't tell him that Drew seemed pretty stable already. I wasn't going to cut my own throat by pronouncing him of sound mind before I'd even begun the job. "Temporary is what I'm looking for."

He nodded. "Your background search and credentials check out. My main concern is your lack of experience. You dropped out of college before completing your doctoral degree. You have no practical experience whatsoever."

I tried not to take offense at his less than favorable summary. "That might be true, but I plan to go back to school next semester. I carried a four point oh grade average. I interned at a psychiatric hospital for a year. And, while I don't have actual experience treating patients, we trained in several simulated therapy sessions. I learned a great deal, and if I do say so myself, I have a knack for the field."

He picked up a pen, flipping it back and forth between his fingers. "When I was a boy, I played doctor. Would you want me to operate on you, Ms. Jackson?"

I smiled. "I hardly think the games you played as a child have anything to do with my abilities, Mr. Breckenridge."

"That may be so. But my concern is that my brother be in capable hands. That he will improve, rather than regressing due to the bumbling attempts of a novice."

Once more ignoring his insults, I sat up straighter in my chair and looked him in the eye. "I can assure you, I'm up to the challenge."

His mouth pulled down in a frown. "I'm not certain you are. I don't believe you're the right person for the job."

My shoulders tensed. Had I actually come all this way, had my hopes raised only to be rejected by this self-righteous, arrogant ass? Joanne led me to believe the job was practically mine and this interview was nothing more than a formality. I guess she hadn't factored in her employer's instantaneous dislike of the applicant she chose.

But then again, how many applicants were there? I was here out of desperation. Not too many people found themselves in my unfortunate circumstances.

Regrouping with more confidence, I rose to my feet and leaned toward him, palms on his desk. "I assume you've considered the fact that it's highly unlikely degreed psychologists will be lining up at your door to take a job as a temporary live-in caretaker and housekeeper at the rate of pay you're offering."

His eyes widened slightly, and he stood also, bringing our bodies too close for my comfort. I straightened away from him.

He crossed his arms and glared. "So, you're dissatisfied with my offer? Yet another reason it would be best if I didn't hire you."

"How many suitable applicants did you get?" Twirling, I swept a hand out, encompassing the room. "They're not exactly crowding in your study for interviews, are they?" I turned back to him. "Looks like I'm the only one here."

He tapped the pen on his palm, averting his gaze down to the surface of his desk as if he couldn't bear to look at me another moment. The lines of tension in his face made me wonder if he'd snap the pen in two.

Finally raising his eyes to mine, he said, "Are you attracted to my brother?"

I drew back in surprise at the disconcerting question. "He-he's a nice- looking guy, but I'm not *attracted* to him. Why do you ask?"

He shrugged. "I'm concerned about the possibility of a romantic entanglement that will further damage his psyche. My brother's condition is serious. He could possibly do himself harm. I intend to ensure that a failed romance doesn't exacerbate his illness."

"I am not the least bit interested in your brother romantically. This is a job. One I need very badly. I'd never do anything to jeopardize that. Regardless, it didn't seem as though your brother had any romantic interest in me." His flirtatious ways indicated he might, but my guess was that he was a ladies' man by nature and the flirting was more a habit than anything else.

He stared at me intently, not speaking for several moments.

Damn. I wouldn't get the job. I'd come all this way for nothing. I'd have to start looking all over...

"You're hired."

My heart pounded so loudly in my ears it took a moment for his words to sink in. *Hired.*

Tension left my shoulders, replaced by elation. "Thank you. You won't be sorry."

He flicked a hand dismissively toward the door. "You may go now."

When I didn't make a move to leave, he said, "Is there anything else?"

"Actually, I'd like to speak with you about something."

He looked pointedly at his study door. "I have work to do. I'd planned to meet with you in the morning at around six before I leave for work. I'll outline your duties and the rules at that time."

So, he expected me to get up at the crack of dawn to speak to him and wouldn't offer me even a minute of his precious time now? Forcing myself to plunge forward, I said, "It will only take a moment."

He sighed heavily. "Fine then. I'll give you five

minutes."

Five minutes? Oh my. I was all aflutter.

He didn't offer me a seat again, nor did he take one himself, as if doing so might encourage a lengthy meeting.

I stretched as tall as my five-foot-four height would allow and linked my hands in front of my body. "I have a…situation. A legal situation. I thought you might be able to help me with it."

"Can you afford to pay me?"

I flinched, taken aback by his rudeness, although I should be used to it by now.

"I was hoping we could work something out. You could perhaps take the fees out of my pay."

"What kind of case is it?"

"I'd like to file a lawsuit against my stepmother. My father recently died. He'd been ill for a very long time. I had no idea he'd changed his will—"

Before I could complete the sentence, he barked out a laugh. The corner of his mouth lifted in the semblance of a smile, but the muscles in his face clenched with censure. "Ah. Money. Doesn't it always come to that? So, let me get this straight. Poor little rich girl thought Daddy would leave his wealth to her. When instead, he left it to the woman he'd pledged his life to, the woman who stood by his side in sickness and health, daddy's girl wants to take it all away from the poor old widow."

I drew in a sharp breath. "How dare you make assumptions about me. You don't even know me."

"Perhaps not. But I have a keen nose for gold-diggers."

"Gold digger?" I couldn't do any more than

stammer out the words. I was flabbergasted, angry, appalled. And, oddly hurt, although why I should care what this Neanderthal thought of me, I couldn't imagine.

I whirled, giving him my back and heading for the door.

When I was halfway across the floor, his voice stopped me. "Aren't you going to give me the details so I can decide if I want to help you?"

Not turning, I tried to keep my tone level. "It's clear you've already formed an opinion about me. I damn sure don't want to retain an attorney who's against me from the beginning. I'll find someone else."

I reached the door.

"Lillian..."

I halted with my hand on the knob, still not facing him.

"Tell me what happened. I don't have a license to practice in Ohio, but I could work with an attorney there if I feel I should take your case." His voice was softer now, almost contrite, but I was too angry to care.

"No, thank you. As I said, I'll find someone else."

Without waiting for a response, I flung the door open and stalked from the room.

Chapter Three

The next morning, after getting up at the ungodly hour of five a.m., I showered and dressed in jeans and a thin red sweater. It was the warmest item of clothing I'd brought. I hadn't anticipated how cold Maine turned in fall.

I arrived in the kitchen at six o'clock sharp as instructed. Clinton was there, his back to me while he poured a cup of coffee from a silver pot. He turned when I entered. He wore dress slacks and a light gray shirt with a dark blue tie. A suit jacket was thrown over the back of one of the chairs.

"Would you like a cup?" He lifted a dark brown mug toward me.

"I don't drink coffee."

"Tea?"

"That would be great."

He stepped back and swept a hand toward the side bar where teabags, scones and muffins were displayed on china serving trays accented with tiny rosebuds and gold trimming. Several colorful ceramic mugs sat next to a carafe.

"That's hot water." He pointed to the carafe.

"Thank you."

Neither of us spoke of last night's encounter, but the tension in the air, the way he stiffly held his shoulders, told me he hadn't forgotten it any more than

I had.

I poured steaming water and dropped in a citrus tea bag. The comforting scent of lemons and oranges soothed my nerves. I chose a cinnamon muffin and returned to the table, taking a seat across from my new boss.

His perpetual frown in place, he said, "I know Joanne told you a little about your duties when she spoke with you on the phone. I'd like to reiterate them and make certain you understand what's expected of you. And, that you understand the rules."

Rules. Made it sound as though I were under house arrest.

"Yes, please." I took a tentative sip of tea. Hot, but delicious. "I need as much information as possible so that I can help your brother." *And so that I don't piss you off*, I silently added.

"You'll be required to conduct daily therapy sessions with Andrew and keep an eye on him when you're not in session. You'll also be expected to help Joanne with the cleaning. She's not able to keep up with it as she once did."

I was amazed that she'd ever kept up with cleaning this enormous house. Surely, it was too much for one person. The fact that she kept this house in order for a short time was mind-boggling. "I'll be happy to do whatever I can to help."

"Your main focus should be Andrew. He has deep-seated issues that manifest in various ways." He bit into a scone and chewed, then took a drink of coffee. "He can be charming, and he's intelligent, but he's also fragile, even self-destructive. It's important that he feels you're on his side, that you're here to listen to him.

21

But…" He raised his eyes to mine and narrowed his scrutiny, his greenish gaze piercing in its intensity. "That's as far as it goes. I meant it when I said there should be no romantic entanglements. For my brother, it could be…" He paused. A quick flash of pain came over his expression, then disappeared just as quickly before he continued, "…devastating."

"Did something happen? A relationship that went wrong?"

He hesitated, scowling into his cup. "There was a woman Drew cared about a great deal. They were engaged to be married. It ended badly."

"And?" When he didn't respond right away, I continued, "If you fill me in, I might be better able to help Andrew."

He lifted his head and met my eyes. "I suspected that she was using Drew. I offered her a payoff to leave."

My mouth dropped open. "You bribed your brother's fiancée?"

"I did. She took it."

A pang of sympathy shot through me. Drew's resentment toward his brother was beginning to make sense. "You destroyed his relationship? And he knows this?"

"Yes." He pushed to his feet. "But, if she loved him, would she have taken the money or would she have told me to go to hell?"

She would have told him to go to hell, just like I wanted to. But her actions didn't excuse what Clinton had done. My blood heated, but I kept my voice steady. "Is there anything else I should know?"

A wry grin touched his mouth. "Isn't that enough?"

He took his suit jacket from the chair back and shrugged it on. "I'll see you this evening."

"Before you go…"

Already at the door, briefcase in hand, he stopped and waited.

"I need to go shopping. I wasn't quite prepared for the cold weather. Would it be possible for me to ride into town with you?"

He frowned and looked down at his watch. "The shops aren't open yet. Joanne's husband, Hank, can take you. Let her know I said it was okay."

Yes, master… The words almost slipped out, but career suicide was not on my to do list for the day.

"Thank you."

He acknowledged my words with a brief nod and strode out the door.

****

Hank wasn't nearly as talkative as his wife. We drove in silence to town, which suited me just fine. Gave me time to process the strange circumstances I'd found myself in. The odd family I was about to entangle my life with. Did I need a job this badly?

My stepmother's face rose in my mind. At the funeral, before we'd even buried my father, she'd cornered me. Her lips tight with triumph, she'd told me I was broke. That, unless I could pay the remainder of the tuition myself, I'd have to leave school. I'd been working to help with living expenses, but there was no way I could afford the tuition. Even with my partial scholarship. My heart had been so heavy with grief, my thoughts on my sweet father lying in the casket at the front of the church, that I hadn't properly processed her words until later.

"We're here."

Hank's voice broke into my reverie. I looked out the window, and awe replaced the sadness of my earlier thoughts. It seemed as though I'd been dropped into the midst of a fairy tale. Blue water stretched out behind rows of quaint shops with roughhewn signs etched with the names of various businesses. Old-fashioned lampposts stood on every corner. Time seemed not to have touched Shoal Harbor.

"You gettin' out or what, missy?" Hank barked.

"Oh, yes. Sorry."

I climbed from the car, and he grunted. "I'll be right here in two hours. That enough time for a female to get 'er shoppin' done?"

I wasn't much of a shopper. I could get it done in half an hour. But I also wanted time to explore. Time to breathe away from the stifling atmosphere of Breckenridge Manor.

"That will be perfect. Thank you."

He grunted once more and drove away.

Chilly wind nipped at my skin through the light jacket I wore as I strolled along the sidewalk, but I was too enthralled with the town to care. I had never seen anything like this in Cincinnati. Thinking of home reminded me I'd yet to reach Brooklyn. Digging around in my purse, I pulled out my cell and dialed.

"Lily? It's about time." Brooklyn's voice held a hint of reprimand that quickly dissolved into excitement. "So, did you get the job? What's it like? What are the people like? I've always wanted to go to Maine. Is it like Stephen King describes it?"

I laughed, my heart warming at the familiar chatter. Picturing her cheery expression caused a lump of sadness to rise to my throat. How could I miss her already? I'd only been gone two days. "I did get the job. It's amazing here. Yes, just like Stephen King describes it. The people are, well..." How to put my impressions in words? I decided to go with vague. "Andrew is nice. His brother, my boss, is kind of a jerk."

"Are they hot?"

I chose my words carefully. "They're both nice-looking."

"Wow. So, you could hook up with one of them. Cool."

I grinned. Brooklyn commanded attention wherever she went and had guys falling at her feet. For her, hooking up with one of them would be second nature. "No. I can't *hook up* with either of them. One is my patient, one is my boss. Geez, Brooklyn. I'm not here for a fling. I'm here to work."

"Can't a girl have some fun?"

"Not that kind of fun." I paused in front of a shop with a parasol-shaped sign hanging above a pink and teal awning. "However, I'm about to go into this adorable little store called Pink Lady Apparel. *Shopping* fun will have to do. Listen, I need to run. Just wanted to let you know I made it here and got the job."

"Okay. I'm happy for you. Call me every day and keep me posted."

"I can't call every day. Not only will I be busy with my job, but the house where I'm staying doesn't have cell service."

"What?" Her shriek pierced my ear. "How will you survive? Ugh. Just message me on Facebook."

I grimaced. "No computer either."

"So, you're basically in hell."

I chuckled. "Not quite that bad. I'll call you as often as I can, how about that?"

We said our goodbyes, and I slipped the phone back in my purse and opened the door to the shop. A bell tinkled when I went inside. The store was small, crowded with racks of clothing and displays of scarves, jewelry, hats, and shoes. A woman who looked to be in her early fifties with gray-streaked red hair and dancing brown eyes met me at the door.

"You're new," she said. "Tourist? We don't get many tourists this time of year." She put her hands on her hips and narrowed her eyes. Before I could respond, she said, "Oh. Yes. You must be Drew's new nanny. How do you like it so far?" She stuck her hand out. "I'm Martha."

Her chattiness in contrast to Hank's brevity had my head spinning. I shook her hand. "Lillian—Lily Jackson. Pleased to meet you. It's—I'm not sure what to think. I've been here less than twenty-four hours."

"Hold onto your hat, honey, you're in for a bumpy ride." Her pleasant expression darkened momentarily. "After the awful mess with Drew and that girl…"

"Girl?" This was the second mention that a woman might have played a part in Drew's issues.

Martha shrugged. "I talk too much. But you'll find out soon enough. Drew was engaged to a girl. He was over the moon for her. She dumped him, and the poor guy hasn't been the same since."

"Someone here in town?" Hopefully, she was a tourist and was long gone. It couldn't be easy for Drew to continually run into a woman who'd broken his heart.

"Name's Melanie Ross. She was from here but disappeared right after she broke up with Drew. Far as I know, no one's heard from her since."

"Really? She's missing?"

Martha shook her head. "I don't know. She's gotta be somewhere, right? The police investigated, but I don't think anything ever came of it. Girl like her, no telling. She might have run off with some guy who had more money than Drew and didn't have a brother who—" She clamped her lips together and smiled with gaiety that seemed forced. "Listen to me, rattling on. Sorry 'bout that. Now, what can I do for you?" Her gaze raked over me. "You probably need some winter clothes, am I right? Where are you from? Let me guess. Wherever it is, it's not as cold as here. I've got just the thing."

She turned and marched toward the back of the store. Trying to hide my disappointment at only getting a morsel of such a juicy story—and feeling slightly ashamed that, as a therapist, I'd been ready to listen to gossip about my patient—I followed her to a rack of sweaters and pants and jackets. Plowing through the hangers like a woman on a mission, she swiped an occasional garment off the rack. When her arms were loaded down, she passed the bundle to me. "Try these on." She cocked a thumb over her shoulder. "Dressing room is in the back."

Since I wasn't crazy about shopping, and since she seemed to know more about what I needed than I did, and since she had this take-charge attitude that brooked no argument, I did as she instructed.

I tried on half a dozen sweaters, checking the cost on each. Although they weren't outrageously priced, they were outside my meager budget. I could afford maybe three or four, but I wouldn't be able to get any of the pants. I'd have to stick with the jeans and Capris I'd brought. What was I thinking? Carpi pants in Maine in November?

I exited the dressing room and laid the clothing in two different stacks on the counter. The one I was leaving behind was much taller.

"I'll take these," I told Martha, pointing to the four sweaters I'd chosen.

She peered at me shrewdly. "You need more than this. I'll open an account for you. Once you start earning a paycheck, you can make payments to me. Did they all fit?"

I nodded.

"Okay then." She plucked a hoodie and three more sweaters from the pile, along with a black pea coat I'd fallen in love with as soon as I'd wrapped its warmth around me. After adding a few pairs of pants to my 'keep' pile, she nodded in satisfaction. "Did you drive?"

"No. Hank dropped me off. He's picking me up in…" I looked at the time on my cell phone. My estimate was almost exact. It had taken me thirty-two minutes in the store, and some of that had been due to Martha's chatter. "…an hour and a half."

"Joanne's Hank? Did he talk your leg off?" She guffawed at her own joke. "If you want to do more shopping, or just look around, I can hold these for you here."

"That would be great." I smiled, touched by her kindness.

When I stepped outside, my eye caught a wooden

sign that read Seafarer's Tavern. Sebastian's bar, I remembered Drew saying. I crossed the street and went in.

A top forty song played over the speakers, and the smell of seafood hung in the air. A waitress in a red and white uniform wove between wooden tables, holding a tray aloft before stopping to place the plates in front of a couple seated at one of the few occupied tables. The waitress glanced up at me, a hint of hostility in her expression. Her customers gave me a similar look.

From behind the bar, Sebastian saw me and smiled that crooked, bitter smile of his. "Have a seat."

I settled on one of the stools, and he handed me a menu adorned with photos of swordfish and lobsters.

"So, did the Breckenridges scare you away yet?" He asked.

"No. Not at all." Gesturing discreetly behind me, I indicated the people in the dining room. "What's with them?" I whispered. "Did I do something to piss them off?"

Sebastian shrugged. "You did. But not on purpose. You're an outsider."

"Seriously? Do they treat all tourists this way?" The town was a popular tourist attraction. With the kind of reception I'd received, I wondered how.

"Nah, they've learned to mask their disdain for them since that's how they make a living most of the year. They know you're not a tourist, though. No need for pretense."

I blew out a frustrated breath. "Awesome."

"What can I get for you?"

After the past twenty-four hours, a shot of vodka sounded tempting, but I didn't think I should go back to my new employer all liquored up. "Just club soda with lime."

"What about food?"

My stomach rumbled, reminding me I hadn't eaten anything since I'd picked at the muffin that morning, and it was well past lunchtime. "Yes. Sure. The fish and chips, please."

He pressed buttons on the screen of a computer that sat behind him. He came back with my club soda and slid it across the bar. I took a sip, then said in what I hoped was a nonchalant tone, "So, did you know Melanie Ross?"

His narrowed eyes glinted with anger. "Why?"

I shrugged as though my interest were casual curiosity. From his reaction, Sebastian *did* know her—and either didn't like her or liked her a great deal. "Just curious. I heard she broke up with Drew, then left town. That it's possible she's missing?"

"She's missing, all right." The words came out strained. "Maybe dead."

A chill raced over my skin. "Dead?"

The anger in his eyes faded, replaced with something that looked suspiciously like pain. "I don't know."

I rested my elbows on the bar and leaned forward. "What do you know? About what happened to her?"

He stared at me for a few moments, jaw tight. "Your food should be ready. I'll be right back."

He didn't speak to me when he brought my lunch out. Didn't say another word as I finished eating, then paid my tab.

Although he hadn't given my any information, he'd revealed something in spite of his reluctance to do so. He'd let me know that there was definitely something to learn.

Chapter Four

Drew and I were scheduled for a session at ten a.m. I spent the morning helping Joanne with chores, following instructions that appeared to be reluctantly given. My guess was that her territorial hackles were raised, and she didn't actually *want* my help.

Just before ten, I rapped lightly on Drew's bedroom door.

He opened it, his handsome face alighting with pleasure.

"Good morning." He stepped back and swept his arm outward, inviting me to enter.

"Good morning." I moved past him into the room. "Are you ready to start your session?"

He studied me in silence for a few moments. "That sweater is the exact same shade as your eyes. You look fantastic."

Heat rose to my cheeks. I'd chosen an indigo knit sweater from the new clothes I'd purchased. The appreciation in Drew's eyes made me slightly uncomfortable. He was being much too flirty to his counselor. An indication he wasn't taking therapy seriously. Not a good sign.

"Thank you, Andrew," I said primly, attempting to keep our association at an impersonal level. "Where would you like to conduct our sessions?"

A crooked grin lifted the corner of his mouth. "My

bed's comfortable."

"If that is a joke, it isn't funny." I frowned and looked over his shoulder. His room was huge, larger than mine, and an open door gave me a peek into a sitting room. We couldn't use Clinton's study and the rest of the house wasn't private enough to ensure confidentiality. The sitting room would be perfect. It was time for me to take charge and lead our relationship down the proper path. "How about in there?" I pointed to the open door. "We'll conduct a one-hour session, then take a break. If you feel up to it, we'll speak again after lunch."

The flirtatious expression he'd crafted fled. "Fine. Whatever you say, doctor."

I headed into the room and Drew followed. After settling into a cushy plaid chair that rested caddy-cornered to a matching sofa, I pulled my notebook out of my bag.

"Should I lie down?" Drew asked with a sarcastic note to his voice.

I crossed my legs and rested the notepad on my knee. "Whatever makes you comfortable."

He huffed and dropped down onto the end of the sofa. "So, what now?"

Although I was far from a trained psychologist, I knew enough to establish rapport. Get him to open up. See what had his brother so concerned. In spite of the bipolar diagnosis, Drew's mood seemed fairly level, normal. But that was part of the illness. At times, those suffering from it could function quite well, especially while on medication. However, medication didn't always keep the patient from experiencing a range of euphoric highs to hopeless meltdowns, and anywhere in between.

"Well, now, we talk. Or, you talk, I listen. Is there anything you want to share with me?"

"You mean, reveal all my deep dark secrets? Confirm my brother's analysis that I'm a whack job?"

"No, that's not what I mean. Tell me whatever you'd like to tell me. Would you like to talk about your childhood? About your relationship with your brother? Your time in the institution?"

"How about you ask me what you want to know."

Again, thoughts of Melanie rose, but I brushed them aside. Time enough for that later. If I asked now, I'd be doing so mostly to satisfy my own curiosity.

"Your brother feels you're self-destructive. Can you tell me what makes him think that?"

Drew's mouth pulled down in a grimace. "Probably because he thinks I'm like our mother."

"And your mother was self-destructive?"

He chuckled without humor. "I'd say so. She killed herself." At my gasp, his brows rose. "You didn't know? You'd think if my brother was going to hire you to treat my psychosis, he'd provide a little more background, wouldn't you?"

I agreed but didn't admit it out loud. Anger at Clinton Breckenridge made me tighten my grip on the pen. I bent my head and scribbled a note to cover it. Taking a deep breath, I faced Drew. "Let's talk about that. When did she die?"

"Two years ago. She drowned herself."

My gut ached with sympathy. "I know what it's like to lose a parent. I'm sorry."

He shrugged. "What can you do, though, right?" The pain in his face eased, but his smile seemed forced.

"Did you hear about the curse attached to this house?"

"No," I lied. Maybe if I let him open up about that, he'd also open up about his grief over losing his mother—and perhaps Melanie. Were his feelings about losing two such important women within a few years part of the self-destructive tendencies his brother mentioned? "Tell me about it."

"Over the past century and a half, most all Breckenridge women have died tragic deaths—some at their own hand. A legend grew with the townspeople after my great-great grandmother drowned. Twenty years before, her own mother was shot and killed during a train robbery. Legend has it that Breckenridge Manor is cursed. Or—technically, the Breckenridges themselves are. They say that falling in love with a Breckenridge man is a death sentence."

I shivered. The words were said lightly, but there was an underlying truth—maybe a warning?—attached to them.

"You seem unhappy here. Why haven't you just left?" As soon as the question was out of my mouth, I regretted it. If I were going to be a therapist, I had to think before I spoke, and definitely before I offer potentially harmful advice. For all I knew, Clinton might be right. Maybe he wasn't a controlling, unreasonable ogre. Maybe Drew did have severe mental problems.

"Go where?" Drew scoffed. "My brother would have me put back in the sanitarium. He controls the family fortune." He leaned forward and clasped his hands loosely between his knees, flashing his disarming smile. "How far do you think I'll get on my good looks and charming personality?"

****

My afternoon session with Drew was less productive than the morning had been. He spent most of the hour evading my questions and flirting. Frustrated, I ended early, then helped Joanne with the housework. She disappeared for nearly an hour, leaving me to my own devices. Apparently, she was more accepting of my help than she'd seemed in the beginning. Just before we wrapped up for the day, I suffered a moment of embarrassment when she found me turning the doorknob to Clinton's study.

"Mr. Breckenridge doesn't allow anyone in his study when he's not here." Her voice lowered with a warning—if not menacing—tone. "Not even me. He keeps highly confidential client files in there."

"I'm sorry," I said, but a thought nagged at me the rest of the afternoon. Was that the only reason his study was off limits? Were there perhaps secrets behind that door he didn't want revealed?

After a tense dinner where little was spoken, I found myself in need of fresh air and activity.

I left the house, taking a stroll along the beach. Light drizzle fell from the sky, and I squinted through the mist. I tasted the salt of the sea breeze on my lips, brushing a strand of hair out of my face when the wind picked up. Once again, a low moan carried to me…like the wail of a woman. I halted, the breath whooshing from my lungs. Shivering, I pulled my pea coat tighter around my body. Could the sound really be the cry of the ghosts of Breckenridge women?

Nonsense. I just wasn't used to the terrain. Wasn't accustomed to being near the sea, to the sounds of the island. *But Sebastian is,* a voice inside my head whispered, *and he was the one to point it out.*

"Nonsense," I muttered, this time aloud. I quickened my pace. The noise faded as the wind subsided. That's probably all it was. The wind. Maybe it howled that way because its echo ricocheted off the cliffs.

I approached a ledge that jutted out over the ocean. Climbing up a few rocks, I rested on the hard surface. Looking out over the water—it's glittering surface dappled golden orange from the setting sun—peace settled over me.

I sat there for close to an hour, my eyelids drooping sleepily. A breeze lifted my hair, and with it came the moan once more. This time, much louder. This time, sounding even more like a woman's cry. Goosebumps broke out over my flesh, and I came full awake. *It's the wind, nothing more than the wind.* Only half convinced, I scrambled from the ledge and headed back to the house.

The house was silent, darkened by evening shadows. Joanne had likely gone home, and Drew was probably in his room. A guy his age shouldn't spend so much time closeted inside. He didn't even have a computer or television in there. What did he do with his time?

Crossing the foyer, I looked down the hall to see a light on beneath the study door. Although a confrontation with the surly master of the house was the last thing I wanted, it needed to be done. Steeling my resolve, I marched down the hall and knocked.

"Yes?" Clinton's voice filtered through the door, impatient, and anything but welcoming.

"It's Lily. May I speak with you?"

Silence. Was he going to ignore me? I stood uncertainly, wavering between knocking again, entering without permission, or fleeing. Before I could decide, his voice came to me again.

"Come in." Not any more welcoming, in spite of the invitation.

I opened the door and stepped inside. He stood from behind his desk.

"What can I do for you?" A lock of chestnut hair fell over his forehead, but not far enough to cover the frown lines.

"I wanted to speak with you about Drew." He waited, and I took a deep calming lungful of air. "I have a bit of insight I'd like to share."

He gestured to a chair across from his desk. "Please. Have a seat. I'm anxious to hear your analysis after one session."

I remained standing. "Two sessions," I corrected in an overly sweet tone. "I don't exactly have an analysis, but I do think you could adjust your attitude toward him just a bit."

"My attitude? In what way?"

"You treat him like a child. He's a grown man. I feel you should give him a little more respect. More freedom and responsibility. He's twenty-nine years old and doesn't have a job. Doesn't do anything except hang out inside this pris—" I stopped just short of saying 'prison.' "This house."

He quirked a brow. "Is that right? More responsibility and freedom? Freedom to make his own decisions? Like the choices he made when he was in the institution?"

"What choices were those?"

He stood and looked out the window where I glimpsed a startling view of the sun lowering behind the ocean, streaking the sky with an array of crimson and purple hues. Keeping his back to me, he said, "He didn't tell you?"

"He didn't talk about his time there." But it was clear I needed to find out. I made a mental note to obtain his records from the sanitarium. I needed objective answers that weren't filtered through the perceptions of either brother.

He nodded and faced me once more. His eyes narrowed. "What did he talk about?"

"I'm sorry. I can't say. It would compromise the doctor patient confidence."

The condescending smirk that I was beginning to realize preceded an insult curled his lip. "It's not like you're a doctor."

I forced my voice to be cool, controlled. "Regardless, Drew trusts me with his confidence. I won't betray that trust."

"Maybe you should remember who pays your salary."

I lifted my chin. "Maybe you should remember you hired me to help your brother. More betrayal is the last thing he needs, especially by someone he's starting to trust."

His brows lifted, and I caught a brief hint of some emotion—admiration perhaps—light his eyes for a moment, then it was gone. "Understood. I shouldn't have asked."

I was speechless for several seconds, not certain I'd heard him correctly. "Was that an apology?"

This time, a hint of a genuine smile surfaced.

"Maybe. Don't get used to it." He gestured toward the door. "If that's it, I have work to do."

"Can I ask you something?" Before he could refuse, I continued, "What made you so…impervious, so controlling? I know you lost your father when you were young. I imagine it was difficult to step into the role as head of the household."

"I hired you to treat my brother. Don't attempt to psychoanalyze me."

Whatever respect he'd briefly entertained had fled. I sighed in resignation. "I wouldn't dream of it. As you said, I'm not a licensed psychologist, and I don't have near enough experience to begin to treat someone with your issues."

His eyes widened. "Touché, Ms. Jackson." The smile reappeared.

I clamped my lips to keep from smiling back. "Goodnight, Mr. Breckenridge." I turned and headed out the door, wanting to savor whatever small victory I'd scored.

****

Unable to sleep, I stood on the balcony, breathing in the salty scent of the ocean on the night air. The moon floated in the blue-black sky. The events of the past few days ran through my mind like reels of a bizarre movie. Sebastian, bitter and secretive, his cryptic remarks drawing me toward a mystery while his antagonism pushed me away. Chatty Martha, the only friendly person I'd met since my arrival. Joanne, who was polite, but not necessarily warm. Such a contrast to her grumpy, close-mouthed husband. Andrew—a young man with either severe issues, or simply a by-product of his past and his controlling brother. The brother. His disdain for me was evident, yet he'd given me the job. Was it because he had at least a little faith in my abilities or because he'd had no other choice?

Both attractive men, although I had no actual interest in either of them. Which was good, considering I was one's therapist and the other's employee. And, considering I wouldn't be here permanently. As soon as I earned enough money to fight my stepmother for my inheritance—and Clinton was satisfied his brother's mental health was a little more secure—I'd be gone.

I had a sudden urge to call Brooklyn, to make contact with someone familiar. To be warmed by her enthusiasm, to have her brightness chase away my gloom. Since that was impossible at the moment, I tried not to think about her—about home.

A part of me would hate leaving this beautiful land. The night stretched out before me in an unending blanket of velvety darkness, its only light the sparkles of moon glinting on the surface of the water. I closed my eyes, drawing in a deep, soothing breath.

My tranquility was shattered when a tortured moan broke the silence.

Chapter Five

I jumped, my heart beating so fast I thought I might be having a heart attack. The ghost? No. The sound had been male. And it wasn't coming from outside.

Drew.

I rushed out of my bedroom and down the hall to his. The moans grew louder when I reached his door.

"Drew?" I knocked, but the only response was another strangled groan. Hesitating briefly, I turned the knob and entered.

Lights from the window revealed his writhing form on the bed, sheets tangled around his body—his near naked body, clothed in nothing but a pair of boxer briefs. He was sound asleep, obviously in the throes of a nightmare.

I paused uncertainly. Should I wake him? It would be extremely awkward, especially since I hadn't taken the time to throw a robe on over my thin gown. But he was in torment. Making my decision, I rushed to the bed.

"Drew?" I said again, louder this time. He didn't wake. I perched on the edge of the mattress and lightly shook his shoulders. "Drew. Wake up."

His eyes flew open, terror in the green depths. Sweat bathed his skin, and his chest heaved with rapid pants.

"What...?" He ran a hand through his hair. "What

happened?"

I released his shoulders. "You were having a nightmare. Are you okay?"

He took a deep breath and let it out slowly. Closing his eyes, he shook his head as if to rid it of the lingering dream. "I'm fine. Sorry if I woke you."

"You didn't. I was up."

He pulled the sheets over his body. Sitting back against the headboard, he stared at me, an embarrassed grin on his face. "Well, still. Sorry I bothered you."

"You want to talk about it?"

He lifted his arm, resting it against his forehead and turning the underside toward me. A white crisscross web marred the flesh on the inside of his wrist. I gasped in horror.

He whipped his head toward me, then quickly lowered his arm. But it was too late. I'd already seen the scars.

His eyes captured mine, pleading with me not to ask questions.

I hesitated before giving a slight nod. I was his therapist, but I wouldn't force him until he was ready.

Softly, I said, "I'll go back to my room now if you're okay."

"I'm fine." He gave me a flirty grin. "Unless you want to stay and keep me company."

I recognized his attempt at deflecting a discussion about his injury. I smiled back. "Thanks, but I think it's best that I leave."

"Suit yourself. But most of the time when I have a woman in my bedroom, she doesn't want to leave."

I chuckled. "Perhaps. But I assume that, most of the time, they're not your therapist." I rose to my feet.

"Maybe in our next session, we'll delve into your acute shyness and lack of self-confidence."

His white teeth flashed in a grin. "Maybe so. Goodnight, Dr. Jackson."

I smiled back. "'Night, Drew."

I closed the door behind me, then stepped into the hallway and came face to face with Clinton Breckenridge.

He looked from Drew's door to me, his mouth tight with irritation. I flushed, feeling as though I'd been caught at something, even though I was innocent. It didn't help that he was fully dressed, still wearing his suit, while I stood outside his brother's bedroom in my nightgown.

"What were you doing in Drew's room?" His voice was clipped. No preamble, just blunt accusation.

"He—he was having a nightmare."

"And you were there when this nightmare occurred?"

"No. Of course not. I heard him cry out, and I went to check on him. Did you not hear him?"

"I was downstairs until a few moments ago." He scowled in disapproval. "Maybe it would be best if you didn't make late night visits to your patient's room."

"Nothing happened." I thought of the scars. I should be the one confronting *him*. "What happened to Drew?"

"You said he had a nightmare."

"No. Not that. I saw the scars on his wrist."

He heaved a sigh. "What does it look like happened?"

"Like he tried to kill himself."

He shrugged nonchalantly, but the grim expression

on his face was anything but. "Like mother, like son."

The savage pain in his voice took me aback. "Drew told me about that. But he didn't mention his own…" I shook my head. The pain he must be holding inside. I looked up into Clinton's ravaged features. The pain both of them must be holding inside.

His only response was a terse nod. "Our mother was also bipolar. As I'm sure you can understand, I worry he'll end up like she did. He's unstable. Self-destructive. What do you think I've been trying to tell you?"

A rush of anger heated my blood. "*Trying* to tell me? It's not that difficult just to say. But you didn't. You're telling me a little at a time. "

He seemed to consider my words, then dismiss them. "Well, now you know. Goodnight." He brushed past me and disappeared down the hallway.

****

The next morning, Drew sulked on the end of the sofa, not meeting my eyes. The wristbands were back in place. What I'd thought was a fashion statement was actually a way to hide his tortured past.

"Tell me about Melanie."

His head snapped up, his eyes wide with surprise…or pain.

I'd decided to go on the aggressive. I wouldn't be here long, and I wanted to delve into Drew's issues as much as possible. Help him as much as I could before I left. *Left like the other women in his life…*

I shook away the thought. I barely knew him. It wasn't like I could affect him the way his fiancée and mother had.

"Who told you about Melanie?" He asked, his tone

45

wary.

"That's not important. What's important is that *you* tell me about her. What happened between you two?"

His smile was bitter, but his shoulders lifted in a casual shrug. "She didn't love me. She left. End of story."

"Is it? The end of the story? How did you feel about that?"

He scoffed. "I was thrilled, elated." His voice held overdramatized incredulity. "I mean, how else would I feel about the only woman I ever loved crushing my heart?"

"I bet that was very difficult. How did you react when she told you?"

"She didn't tell me. She told Clinton. He delivered the news. The note."

"What did it say?"

Pain shadowed his eyes. "That she was leaving. That it was over between us."

"How did that make you feel?"

Jumping to his feet, he stalked to the window, turning his back to me. "Good God, are you some kind of caricature or something? Ask me something real, not 'how did that make you feel.'" He mimicked a nasally feminine voice. Whirling, he strode back over, looming above me. "Ask me if I believe she really left of her own accord. Ask me what I think really happened."

"No." I didn't want to ask him. Didn't want to know. Not if it increased my growing suspicion of Clinton Breckenridge.

"No? Are you afraid of the answer?" He scowled down at my lap. "Why aren't you writing this down? Compiling notes on the nutcase you were hired to babysit." He swiped at my notebook, knocking it to the floor.

"Drew, you don't—"

"If you're not going to ask, I'll tell you." He crossed his arms. "I'm not sure she took the payoff. I'm not sure that she left here of her own free will. Or, for that matter, that she left here at all."

I swallowed back a cold knot in my throat. "What do you mean?"

"I assume if you heard about her at all, you heard she disappeared. Clinton hated her. Why don't you ask him what happened?"

****

I didn't see Clinton Breckenridge for the next few days. I'd established a pattern that prevented me from crossing his path. A late breakfast, then housework in the morning. A session with Drew before lunch. Then a walk along the beach where I'd settle on the ledge I'd discovered my second day here.

The view was the most stunning from this vantage point, the old lighthouse no more than twenty feet away. Although the tower was weathered with age, and the gabled red roof was faded to a light salmon color, I thought it beautiful. I'd found my own little oasis where I could relax—a place to gather my thoughts. Then, after lunch, there would be another session with Drew.

One morning I arrived at breakfast and ran into Clinton. It was the first time I'd seen him since Drew voiced his suspicions regarding Melanie Ross. Although uneasy, I was curious about what had actually happened. I found it unlikely that Clinton Brackenridge was a killer, in spite of his nasty temper. Melanie Ross was obviously intent on finding fortune and had probably moved on to her next target. But with all the unanswered questions…

It was a Saturday, and he was dressed casually in a long-sleeved olive green thermal shirt and worn jeans that somehow made him seem less intimidating. More human.

After a brief greeting, he said, "I'm going into town. Do you need anything?"

I did. I needed to find out some answers to the odd facts I'd learned. Martha would be the one to have them.

"Actually, may I go with you?"

He frowned. "Why?"

I gritted my teeth. "I need a few—personal items."

He seemed to consider it, then nodded, although a bit reluctantly.

After a quick breakfast, we headed out to the car. The drive to town was silent, the air so thick with tension I could taste it. Why didn't he like me? What had I ever done? Was it true, he just didn't like women? I studied him from the corners of my eyes, the strong hands on the wheel, the defined muscles beneath the thin material of his shirt. He enjoyed women, Drew had said. Unbidden, a thought crept into my head. *I'm sure women enjoy him too…*

Clinton glanced at me, catching me staring. My face heated, and I turned to look out the window.

"Have you spoken with an attorney yet?"

I shook my head. Truthfully, I hadn't even thought to. "No. I wasn't certain where to start."

"I can give you some names. None of their offices will be open today, but you can call them on Monday."

A reminder that he wasn't going to help me. Good

enough. I didn't want his help. My stepmother's hateful face rose in my vision. Okay. I wanted his help. But no way in hell would I ask again.

We arrived in town, and he turned to me. "Where do you need to go?"

"The drugstore will be fine."

Surprisingly, he pulled into the parking lot to drop me off rather than making me walk from wherever he needed to go. "I'll be finished in forty-five minutes. Meet me here."

Yessir, I almost said aloud. Wisely, I simply nodded and fumbled the door open, then scrambled from the car.

I went into the drug store and found an ATM to cash my check, then glanced around the store. A middle-aged woman behind the counter peered at me suspiciously. "What can I do for you?"

"I just need to pick up a few things. I can find them on my own."

An unfriendly tilt of her head was the only response she gave.

I picked up body lotion and styling mousse, then hurriedly paid for my purchases, anxious to escape the hostile atmosphere. Stepping out into the chilly wind, I took a deep, cleansing breath and headed for Pink Lady Apparel.

Martha's usual friendly smile warmed me after the chill of my reception a few moments ago. "They haven't devoured you yet?"

"Who?"

"The Breckenridges or the townspeople. You're made of heartier stuff than you look."

"No, I'm still in one piece." I smiled. "I received

my first check. I wanted to make a payment to you."

"Well, aren't you little Miss Responsible. I knew I could trust you."

"Thanks. I appreciate the vote of confidence."

She took my money, and I searched my mind for a way to open a conversation about the troubling facts I'd learned. I didn't want to bring up Clinton's bribe to Melanie, so I chose a less volatile topic.

"Do you believe in ghosts?" I asked.

Martha's eyes sparkled. "I do. Do you?"

"No. I mean, I never did before. But Drew told me there was a legend about the ghosts of Breckenridge women. Sometimes, I think I can hear their cries."

"Oh sure," she nodded matter of factly. "Certain times, when the wind blows just right, you'll hear them."

An icy chill traveled down my spine. "You really believe that's what the sound is? Ghostly cries?"

"What else would it be? Tragic deaths like the Breckenridge women. Their spirits can't rest."

I couldn't believe I was listening to this, that I was half-believing it. "Tragic deaths?"

Martha nodded slowly. The smile faded from her face. "Clinton and Drew's great-grandmother was murdered. Their great-grandfather was a suspect, but nothing was ever proven. No one paid for the crime. Their grandmother died in an accident at the lighthouse. Then, as you probably know, their mother committed suicide. Yep. A long line of horrible deaths in that family."

"Oh my God. Are you serious?"

"Would I joke about something like that?" I drew back at the uncharacteristic sharpness in her tone. Her voice softened. "Sorry. It's just so sad. You'd think women would steer clear of the Breckenridge men, but they're drawn to them like flies to a whale carcass." She chuckled "Can't say as I blame 'em. If I was twenty years younger, I'd give 'em a go, in spite of the risk."

My brows rose in surprise. "Is that right?"

She winked. "You bet. It'd be worth it, don't ya think?"

"I—uh. Well, I'm employed by Mr. Breckenridge, so I don't feel comfortable—"

She let out a boisterous laugh. "Don't get your panties in a bunch. I was just having some fun."

I smiled. "It seems Sebastian doesn't share your affection for the Breckenridges. He actually despises them."

Her shoulders lifted in a shrug. "Yeah, well, he blames them for something that ain't their fault. He fell for a hussy, and she stomped on his heart. He needs to put the blame where the blame lies. With Melanie."

"Melanie? Sebastian was in love with her?"

"He was engaged to her before she set her sights on Andrew. Now, he's turning into a bitter man. Time for him to move on, I'd say. He just can't seem to let go. I saw him confront Clinton a few days after Melanie took off. Accused him of funny business. They were right out there on the sidewalk." She pointed to her front window. "I heard part of what they said but couldn't hear it all. Sebastian said something like, 'You'll never get away with it' and Clinton said, 'Neither will you.'"

"Get away with what?"

"I don't know. Something to do with Clinton paying her to leave, I guess."

So, that was why Sebastian hated the Breckenridge brothers. Drew had stolen Melanie away from him and Clinton had paid her to leave town. Had he also hated Melanie? Had he wanted to punish her for jilting him? I shuddered. The more I learned, the less I knew. And the less I trusted the people I'd met since my arrival in Shoal Harbor.

Chapter Six

I suggested that Drew and I hold our next therapy session outside. Maybe being outdoors would lift his spirits...and mine. The sun was hidden behind a bank of clouds, making the air cooler than usual for this time of day. Jagged cliffs were shrouded in a purple haze. That same shade was reflected in the surface of the water, above which a seagull swooped across the deep blue sky.

I wrapped my jacket around me as we walked along the moisture-packed sand.

Drew shoved his hands in his pockets and slanted me a look. "I want to thank you for what you've done for me. It's been a long time since I've felt like I've had a friend."

I smiled, brushing a strand of hair from my face. "I'm glad the therapy is helping."

"I don't mean in a professional sense. I like you, Lily. I haven't met anyone who made me feel so... I don't know...so safe...so cared for."

Dread settled in my gut. "Drew, I—"

"Let me finish. No one has ever made me feel that I matter. That my opinions matter, you know? Even Melanie. She wasn't all that interested in my wants. My needs. I know you're paid to help me. But I can also tell that you truly care."

"I do care. I want to see you better. That's why it's

important that you share your past with me. Share the experiences that brought you where you are today." After pausing a moment to let my words register, I said, "Are you ready to tell me why you tried to take your own life?"

He halted and stared down at me. "Just for today, can we put all that out of our minds? Can we let this therapy session be about just letting go? Relaxing and forgetting all the bad, just for a little while?"

Unable to resist his cajoling, I relented. "Sure. I could use some of that myself."

A relieved smile lit his face. "Hey, I know what you'd like. Come on."

I didn't protest when he took my hand and led me farther down the beach. We stopped at a small cove where a rowboat bobbed in the water. "Want to take her out?"

I raised my brows. "You're kidding, right? That little thing? In the sea?"

"Of course. We won't go very far out. It's safe, I promise."

I frowned up at the sky. "It looks like it might storm."

"Nah. If it starts, we'll come back right away."

Since the ferry ride, I'd wanted to be back on the water. But, this wasn't exactly what I had in mind. I was thinking something bigger, sturdier. I nibbled at my bottom lip. Drew looked so eager, I couldn't disappoint him. "Okay." I shrugged. "Why not."

Drew helped me inside, then took the oars, steering us away from the beach. His hair whipped around his forehead, and his eyes sparkled, making him look like a child on Christmas morning. I hadn't seen such happiness, such relaxation in his expression since I'd met him. Maybe putting off the therapy session was exactly what he needed.

We rowed toward the lighthouse. It stood sentinel, lonely. I shuddered. An inanimate object couldn't be lonely, but its isolation gave that impression. It called to me somehow, as if we were kindred spirits. Because it was abandoned, as I'd been?

"It's so beautiful, so haunting."

I didn't realize I'd spoken aloud until Drew said, "Yeah. Lighthouses seem to be a source of fascination for a lot of people. That one hasn't been functional since the early sixties."

Martha had said Drew's grandmother died there. Was that why it was no longer in use?

As if he'd read my mind, Drew said, "My grandmother died in an accident there in 1957 when my father was a baby. My grandfather was the lighthouse keeper, and she sometimes took over to help him out. She fell down the stairs. No one knows exactly what happened, since she was alone. My grandfather never got over it. He died five years later, and the lighthouse was closed." He shrugged. "Of course, with the use of radio technology and automated lighthouses, the keepers were no longer needed anyway."

"Wow, sad story. Intriguing, too. I've been curious since I got here. I'm one of those people fascinated with lighthouses."

He grinned. "Well, I'm happy to play tour guide."

I rested back against the bow. It was nice being out here with Drew. I had no romantic feelings about him, but I could see us being friends. Which was also a bad idea. I was a psychologist—sort of.

Apparently spurred by my attentiveness to his lighthouse story, Drew went on to tell me several facts about the history of Shoal Harbor, about how his family had been there for generations and how his great, great, great-grandparents had been instrumental in establishing the fishing industry in the area, which had eventually led to the island's success as a booming tourist attraction.

We'd been out for over half an hour when the wind shifted, and the sky darkened. With it, the breeze chilled further.

Tension tightened my muscles. "What's going on?"

"Just a sea squall."

"A storm?" I couldn't control the fear in my voice. "But you said it wasn't going to."

"It's nothing."

"How can you know that? Bad weather can get out of hand in no time. Let's go back."

"It'll be fine." He spoke soothingly. "We'll go back in a minute. I want to show you—"

"Now," I interrupted. "Let's go back now."

A streak of lightning ripped through the sky, and I let out a small yelp.

Drew peered at me curiously. "Are you okay?"

My stomach fluttered. I took in a deep breath. "I—I know it's silly, but I'm afraid of storms."

"Why?"

"Are we on our way back?" I glanced around, trying to gauge our location and whether or not we were getting closer to the beach.

"Hey." He let go of one of the oars and reached out to squeeze my hand. "I won't let anything happen to you. I promise, you'll be fine."

"Please just row, okay?"

"Yeah, sure." He released my hand and grabbed the oar, rowing us toward the beach. "Do you want to tell me why you're so scared?"

I bit my lip. On one hand I did, on the other, it was difficult to talk about. Even though it happened fifteen years ago, the images were never far from my mind.

Gripping my hands together in my lap, I said, "When I was twelve, my parents and I were driving home from a trip to Memphis to see relatives." The memory brought tears to my eyes. I brushed them away and swallowed. "We were halfway home when the weather turned nasty. Rain pounded down. A huge clap of thunder shook the entire car." My stomach muscles clenched. I could feel the pull of the vehicle as my father fought to keep us on the road...as the water rose around us...as the tires lost their traction.

"Hey. You don't have to talk about it."

I snapped my head up. I'd almost forgotten Drew was there. "The car spun out of control. We crashed into a guardrail. The impact was at the front passenger side. Where my mother was." My lips trembled, and I sucked in a lungful of air. "She died."

"I'm so sorry," he said.

I nodded but didn't respond. My vocal cords no longer seemed to be working. The storm was coming. The sky had turned a menacing blue-black and flashes of lightning spiked across the water.

Just as we reached the beach, the heavens opened up and dumped a flood of rain. Drew climbed from the boat, securing it quickly. He took hold of my hand, and we raced up the beach. Freezing wind chilled me, and I shivered uncontrollably.

We ran together to the house. When we reached the porch, a clap of thunder rattled through my bones. I screamed

"Hey, hey. It's okay." Drew took my face in his hands, staring into my eyes. "You're okay. I've got you. You're safe."

I nodded, drawing in a breath. I wouldn't cry. Not in front of my patient. Not again. "Thank you."

He still held my face in his hands. His gaze dropped to my mouth. I knew what was going to happen before it happened. I should have stopped it, but before I could form a plan, his lips pressed against mine. They were warm on my cooled skin, but other than that, I felt nothing. Part of me was relieved to discover my patient elicited not even the slightest hint of attraction. The other part felt guilty as hell for allowing it to happen.

I lifted my hands to his and was about to pull back when the front door opened. I tugged away, and turned my head, hoping to see Joanne, or Hank, or a vicious, rabid animal. Anyone other than Clinton Breckenridge.

He loomed in the doorway, the light behind him spilling over his furious expression. Arms crossed over his chest, he glowered at me, then at his brother.

****

I stood in the middle of Clinton's study, my hands linked in front of me. He hadn't invited me to sit. He stood behind his desk, his face dark with anger that rolled off him in waves. I wanted to defend myself, but I was completely in the wrong, so I remained silent. He was going to fire me. I knew it. But I wouldn't speed up the inevitable. I waited.

"I thought I made it clear from the beginning that

there were to be no romantic entanglements."

"I know. It wasn't what it looked like. He was trying to comfort me."

He barked a disbelieving laugh. "Right. I've seen comfort, and that wasn't what I witnessed between you and my brother."

I didn't respond. There wasn't much I could say to his accurate assessment.

"The last thing Drew needs is for another woman to take him for a ride. To throw herself at him, to screw with his head."

"Is that what you think I did?"

"It's what I *saw*."

"Your brother kissed *me*. It took me off guard. I'll admit, I let him, but I certainly didn't initiate it."

He was silent for several seconds. I shifted uncomfortably, still wet and chilled. Miserable.

"You shouldn't encourage his affections."

"I didn't mean to. I didn't do anything."

He came around the desk and walked slowly toward me. My legs weakened with fear and an unsettling anticipation. He halted mere inches in front of me. I didn't retreat. Lifting my head, I stared into his face.

"You didn't do anything?" His voice was a low murmur, running over my cool flesh. "Not even bat those pretty blue eyes at him? Purse your lips in that flirty little way you have? As though you're begging to be kissed?"

"I—I don't." My throat ached with the effort to speak around the knot. Where I was chilled only moments before, slow warmth now spread through my blood. "I'm not sure what you mean."

He bent his head. Unable to breathe, I stared in fascination while his mouth drew closer.

His lips curved in an indolent smile, and he stepped back, leaving me feeling cold once more, other than the heat rising to my cheeks. I'd thought he was going to kiss me. And I'd have let him. Fury nearly brought tears to my eyes, but I sniffed them back.

He moved behind his desk. "I won't tolerate this kind of behavior from my staff. I should have known I couldn't trust you."

"You *can* trust me," I bit out when I was able to speak. "I *do* have Drew's best interests at heart. And, I know that you do too. That's why I don't understand your hostility since the day I arrived. Why don't you like me?"

"I pay your salary. I don't have to like you."

A pang of hurt in my chest caught me unaware. I swallowed, infusing strength in my voice that I didn't feel. "Are you going to fire me?"

His mouth compressed. "Not this time. But if it happens again, you're through. Got it?"

****

The next morning, I had trouble concentrating on my session with Drew. I kept thinking about the kiss, and the almost kiss with Clinton. My disappointment that it hadn't happened. What the hell was wrong with me? How could I be attracted to a man like Clinton Breckenridge?

Brushing the thought aside, I said to Drew, "Don't you think it's time we talked about what happened in the hospital? About your attempted suicide?"

"Not particularly. Why don't we talk about the kiss?"

I sighed heavily. "Drew, that never should have happened. I'm your therapist. It's highly unethical."

"Maybe, but it was nice, right?"

I didn't respond. How could I tell him that it wasn't as nice as the mere *thought* of kissing his brother? He held enough resentment toward Clinton. I wouldn't add that to it.

"Please. Tell me about when you hurt yourself. You need to talk about it with someone."

Tears surfaced in his eyes. He shook his head and cleared his throat. "I was miserable in that place. At my lowest point. I kept thinking about my mother. About how she found a way to escape."

"Escape? In death? What about the hurt she left behind? Would you want to do that to those who love you?"

He laughed bitterly, thumbing tears from his eyes. "Now that she's gone, there's no one left who cares."

"That's not true. Your brother loves you very much."

He rolled his eyes. "Some psychologist you are. He hates me."

"If he hated you, would he go through such lengths to get you well? Wouldn't he have just left you where you were?"

"If he cared about me, would he have gotten rid of the only woman I ever loved?"

By 'gotten rid' I had to wonder if he meant more than the payoff. But I didn't ask. I didn't want to hear about his suspicions of Clinton. Even if they made sense. *Especially* if they made sense.

"I'm sure he thought he was looking out for you."

His eyes took on a faraway expression. As if he

hadn't heard me, he said, "I gave her a necklace. A diamond heart with an emerald in the center."

I sat back, not speaking. Waiting for him to unburden the painful memories he'd kept buried.

"The last time I saw her, she was wearing the necklace. Said she'd never take it off. It meant something to her. *I* meant something to her. I know I did. She wouldn't just leave like that."

I had to wonder how much the necklace was worth. Perhaps that's why she valued it so much.

Or, maybe I was being too cynical. The music box was worth a great deal of money, but that wasn't why I valued it. I'd never met Melanie, yet I was making unfair assumptions. Was she staring at the necklace at this moment? Missing Drew and wishing she'd chosen him over the money? Or, was Sebastian right? Was Drew right? Had something happened to her?

The most disturbing question kept tugging at my mind. Whatever happened, had Clinton Breckenridge been responsible?

****

Later that afternoon, I was returning from my walk when I spotted a man standing near a white pine along the edge of the Breckenridge property. I changed directions, heading toward him. I wouldn't confront him if he seemed dangerous, but I was curious about who he was and what he was doing scoping out the manor.

When I was ten feet away, he turned, and I recognized Sebastian.

He watched me approach with narrowed eyes. "Sebastian, what's going on? What are you doing here?"

His face colored, and he shoved his hands in his pockets. "I came to see you."

I recognized it as a lie right away, but why lie? I crossed my arms and lifted my brows. "Yes? And what can I do for you?"

He looked past my shoulder unseeingly, then at me. "I wanted to apologize for the way I treated you when you came into the bar."

He wouldn't meet my eyes, and he stumbled over the words. I sensed that apologizing was something he rarely did. I also sensed he was less than sincere.

"Would you like to come up to the house for a cup of coffee?"

I waited, the challenge hanging between us. I wasn't sure what I'd do if he accepted. Drew and Clinton were no fonder of him than he was of them. Some devil inside me wanted to gauge his reaction to the offer.

His jaw clenched, and he shook his head. "Thanks, but I have to be somewhere." He peered back at the house. "Do they ever talk about her?"

I didn't have to ask who he was referring to. "I don't feel comfortable discussing the Breckenridges with you, Sebastian."

Still not looking at me, he backed away. "Watch yourself, Lily," he said over his shoulder. He made his way around the edge of the property line, disappearing before I had a chance to inform him that the proper way to deliver an apology was not skulking around someone's home like a criminal.

****

I'd been at Shoal's Harbor for two weeks, and while I was starting to adjust to my new surroundings, I hadn't adjusted to the lack of technology. I longed to speak with Brooklyn, but it would have to wait until my next trip to town. My life in Cincinnati seemed like forever ago. Speaking with my friend would help me feel more connected to home.

I was heading to the ledge when I spotted Drew, standing at the shoreline, staring out over the sea.

"Hello," I said.

He turned and smiled. "Hi there. Fancy meeting you here."

"I always take a walk after lunch. I'm glad to see you're not holed up in your room."

"It's a nice day. Feels good to be outside."

The weather was not as cold as it had been. The sun shone, warming me in spite of the slight nip in the breeze.

"My thoughts exactly."

"I'm sorry about the other day," he said. "About taking you out in a storm. I had no idea what you'd gone through."

"It's okay. Really."

A grin appeared. "How do you feel about having company on your walk?"

"I'd like that a lot. I'll take you to my favorite spot."

He laughed. "You're new to the island, and you already have a favorite spot? Sounds like you're settling in pretty well."

No. I wasn't. I couldn't. I would only be here a short while.

I gave him a smile. "Come on."

He followed behind me, and I led him to the ledge. I turned to look over my shoulder, ready to invite him to climb up with me and enjoy the view.

He hung back, his face drained of color, his eyes filled with stark terror.

"Drew? What's wrong?"

His body trembled. Low sounds of pain emitted from his clenched lips.

"Hey," I said softly, reaching out to take his arm. "What is it?"

He jerked away from me, the moans turning into full blown screams of agony. He doubled over, falling to his knees in the sand.

What on Earth? "Drew, talk to me." I knelt before him. "Look at me. Please tell me—"

The screams intensified. He clutched his middle and rocked back and forth.

"Drew?" A masculine voice bellowed

I whirled to find Clinton striding towards us.

"What's wrong with him?" My voice quavered.

"For God's sake. Are you out of your mind?" Clinton barked.

"What's wrong with him?" I asked again. "What did I do?"

He ignored me. He reached down and took Drew's arm, gently helping him to his feet.

"It's okay," he murmured. "It's okay, buddy. You're all right. Come on. Let's get you inside."

Drew's screams subsided, but his body still visibly trembled. Clinton wrapped an arm around his shoulder, turning him and leading him toward the house. I followed behind, confusion and guilt weighing heavy in my chest. I wasn't sure why I felt guilty, but I'd done something wrong. I just didn't know what. Clinton's soothing words floated back to me, but neither of them acknowledged my presence.

When we reached the porch, Drew halted, turning a ravaged expression up to his brother. "I was there," he choked out. "The day she…" He screwed his eyes shut. Tears squeezed between them. "I saw her jump. I couldn't get to her in time."

Clinton's face blanched as if he'd been punched in the gut. "You were there? And you didn't tell me?"

"I couldn't…" Drew opened his eyes. "Couldn't talk about it."

I stood, rooted to the spot, an unwelcome voyeur in the family drama unfolding. Drew had witnessed his mother's suicide? He hadn't even told me that in session. What kind of therapist was I?

Joanne met us at the door. "What is it? What's happening?"

"Get him to his room, would you?" Clinton asked. "I'll be up to check on him shortly."

After Joanne and Drew left, Clinton turned to me, his expression dark with anger. "How the hell could you?"

"Could I what?"

"You took him to the place where our mother killed herself. She jumped from that very ledge."

I sucked in a breath. "Oh, God. I had no idea. I…" The words wouldn't come. I now knew why I should feel guilty. Although I had no idea, I'd made Drew come face to face with the worst moment in his life.

"Perhaps you should check with me before you expose my brother to even more distress than he's already dealt with, understand?"

I lifted my chin. "If you'd told me that was where his mother—your mother—killed herself, there's no way I would have taken him there."

A muscle jumped in his jaw. He seemed about to say more. Instead, he turned and strode inside the house, leaving me on the porch, alone with my guilt. With the knowledge that I'd never make a good therapist. That I'd done Drew more harm than good. That maybe it was time I left.

Chapter Seven

I stood uncertainly outside Clinton Breckenridge's bedroom door. I owed him an apology. One that hadn't been delivered soon enough.

I hesitated, then taking a deep breath, I steeled my resolve and knocked.

He opened the door, his light blue shirt partially unbuttoned, tie in hand. His brows rose. "Yes?"

"I'm sorry to disturb you, but I wanted to apologize for what happened with Drew."

He frowned. "As you said, I should have told you."

"Yes, but I should have been more in tune with his feelings. Should have picked up on something. Should have pressed him about his mother's death."

"You had no way of knowing."

"Maybe not." I took another deep breath. "I think I should resign. I'm not helping Drew, and I don't want to cause him more heartache."

He narrowed his eyes. "Is that what you want? I thought you needed the job."

"I do." I needed it desperately, but not at Drew's expense. "Drew should have a therapist with more experience. Someone who can provide the help he requires."

He released a heavy sigh and leaned against the doorjamb. "There is no one else. You were right. You were the only applicant. Besides, you have helped him.

He's opening up more with you than he did at the facility. He's getting out of the house. This was a misunderstanding. It's not your fault."

I tried to hide my surprise. Not what I expected from him. But then, I hadn't expected the gentleness he'd shown his brother. Maybe, he wasn't such an ogre after all.

"How's Drew?"

"He's calm now."

"You were wonderful with him."

He looked down at the floor, then back up at me. "I had no idea he was there. That he'd seen her..." He broke off and compressed his lips. "I wish he'd talk to me." Dampness glistened in his hazel eyes.

My heart ached at the show of emotion from this formidable man. He cared deeply for his brother, that much was obvious. I clenched my fists at my sides to keep from reaching out to comfort him. "He's a troubled young man."

A small smile curved his lips. "Young man? He's older than you by a few years."

"I guess he just seems young. Vulnerable." And I'd taken him to the spot where his mother had killed herself. Had Drew heard the cries? Had *I* actually heard them or were they just a figment of my imagination? I looked up at Clinton. "Do you hear the cries when the wind blows?"

He snorted a laugh. "You've been listening to ghost stories."

"I heard them. The moans. It sounds like a woman crying."

"Surely you don't believe that? I suppose you also heard that the women who fall in love with the men in my family meet with a tragic end. Do you believe that?"

"I don't know what I believe." I tried to keep my tone light but didn't quite pull it off. "Just in case, I guess it's a good thing I'll never fall in love with you."

"Because you love my brother?"

My brows rose. "Of course not. He's my patient. You mean because of that one little kiss?"

He smirked. "Was it, Lillian? Just one little kiss?"

The words seemed infused with meaning, although I couldn't grasp their significance. His face was shadowed, the faint light behind him making his eyes look iridescent. The air between us grew heavy with tension, and I struggled to draw air into my lungs. Without realizing I was doing it, I stepped closer. His chest rose, then fell with an expelled breath.

When he spoke, his voice was a hoarse whisper. "You should probably leave. If you don't, I'll invite you in." With a hint of reluctance, he added, "That wouldn't be a good idea."

I swallowed against the knot lodged in my throat and gave a jerky nod. "Goodnight," I said, not moving away.

He stared at me for a moment, neither of us speaking. Or departing. He lifted a hand and ran his thumb down my cheek. His touch was warm and electrifying. I shuddered.

He dropped his hand and heaved another sigh. "Goodnight, Lillian."

****

The next morning, I woke up early, not having slept well. My mind played the scene in Clinton's doorway over and over again. What had it meant? Was he attracted to me? *He enjoys women*, Drew had said. But nothing up to this point indicated he found anything enjoyable about me. Until last night.

Shaking off the thoughts, I threw back the covers and took a quick shower, wishing I had cell service. Being without technology sucked. I couldn't call Brooklyn. Couldn't even Facebook her. Couldn't search for newspaper articles about Melanie Ross.

A burning need to know the truth had taken hold. I wanted Drew's suspicions of his brother laid to rest. Clinton obviously loved him a great deal. Before I left, I would do my best to mend their relationship. I also wanted *my* suspicions about Clinton laid to rest. The man I'd seen caring so tenderly for his brother was not a man who could commit murder.

I almost laughed at my own naivety. I thought of the countless news reports I'd seen of interviews with neighbors of mass murderers, serial killers, rapists. Most of them said the same things. *He seemed so normal. He never acted violent. He taught my children's Sunday School class...*

Murderers rarely revealed their true selves. Not until after they were caught.

I hitched a ride into town with Hank. His non-chattiness was exactly what I needed. I had to focus. I had a mystery to solve.

Hank dropped me off at the library. I called Brooklyn before I went inside, filling her in on what had happened since my arrival.

"So...you think that chick is dead?"

"I have no idea. I'm going in to the library to search for newspaper articles."

"Oh dear God. Tell me you're not going to search

through microfiche or whatever those ancient tomes were called. It's uncivilized enough that you have to go to the *library* to use a computer. Please tell me they at least *have* computers."

"I'm hoping they do. Wish me luck."

Inside, I waited twenty minutes for one of the three computers to become available. Finally, a young guy stood and slung a backpack over his shoulder. I wasn't sure if he was actually finished or if he'd tired of my heavy sighs and pointed looks at the clock on the wall.

I sat in the vacated chair and googled "Melanie Ross," "missing," and "Shoal Harbor." A newspaper article from six months earlier popped up.

A police investigation had gotten nowhere. No suspects. No indication of foul play. Clinton had been forthcoming about paying her off, but the check was never cashed.

I sat back in the chair, chewing on the pad of my thumb. Had there been foul play or had she taken off with someone as Martha suggested? If so, why hadn't she cashed the check?

I looked at the time on the corner of the screen. I had half an hour before Hank would pick me up in front of the library. Hastily, I headed out the door to Martha's shop.

As always, she was happy to see me. I made a payment on my balance, then instigated small talk for a few minutes before I worked up the nerve to broach the topic that was the true reason for my visit.

Infusing my voice with nonchalance, I said, "You know Clinton Breckenridge pretty well. I wonder…have you ever seen him…" I faltered, searching for the right words. None came to me, so I blurted, "Seen him lose his temper?"

Her mouth pulled into a frown. "What are you getting at?"

I shrugged. "I'm just wondering. I mean, with what happened to Melanie Ross. *If* something happened. Well...Clinton was one of the last people to see her."

A dark look came over her expression. "You want to know about Clinton Breckenridge?" Without waiting for my response, she continued, "He would be furious if he knew I was telling you this, but I do know something about him."

"Yes?" I leaned across the counter, waiting breathlessly.

"See these?" She pulled the neck of her sweater down, revealing livid, mottled scars on her clavicle.

I let out a cry and pulled back. Nausea crawled to my throat, and I regretted questioning her. I didn't want to hear more, but it was too late to back out now.

My words came out in a strangled whisper. "Clinton did that to you?"

She smiled without humor and released her sweater, covering the scars. "Is that what you think of him? Do you think he's capable of something like that?"

"I—I don't know him. How would I—"

"My ex-husband did it to me. He used to beat the crap out of me on a regular basis. I was afraid to leave him, afraid not to. One day, he took a knife to me. I finally got the nerve to talk to Clinton. He handled it all. Pro bono. For free, in case you didn't know that."

"I know what pro—"

She cut me off. "So, not only did Clinton see me through my divorce. Protect me from that jerk throughout the proceedings, he convinced my ex to leave the island. Told him he'd drag him back into court once a month if he didn't go. My ex was shady. Had run-ins with the law all too often. He wouldn't have wanted that, so he moved on. Never heard from him again. So, if you want to find out anything bad about Clinton Breckenridge you'll have to go somewhere else. 'Cause you sure won't get it out of me."

Martha's friendliness had fled. Misery nearly choked me. Not only had I made false assumptions about Clinton, I'd alienated the only friend I'd made since my arrival.

"I'm sorry." I wished a hole would open up in the floor and swallow me, but I couldn't be that lucky.

She marched to the door and held it open. "Now if you'll excuse me, I have work to do."

Nodding, I ducked my head and hurried from the store.

****

I slid into the passenger seat, and Hank handed me an envelope. "Picked up the mail. This is for you."

I frowned, taking the letter. The return address was from a law firm in Cincinnati. Odd. I hadn't spoken to anyone about the lawsuit. Had Clinton already contacted someone on my behalf? He was turning out to be some kind of saint, apparently. Perhaps he had.

I tore the seal and pulled out a single sheet of paper. My confusion grew as I read. Beneath my name and address were the words, *RE: In the estate of Marshall Jackson*. My confusion turned to fury when I read further.

Dear Ms. Jackson,

Our firm is handling the above-mentioned estate. It has come to our attention that a music box is missing from the inventory of Heather Jackson's belongings. Our client has reason to believe you might be in possession of said music box.

If you have the item, please contact our office immediately to make arrangements to return it. If we do not hear from you within thirty days, our firm will proceed with legal action against you.

My hands dropped to my lap, the letter fluttering to the floorboard.

How dare she?

Angry tears clogged my throat. The music box was mine. I had a right to *something* from my father. I had a right to a lot more than that, but there was no way I was giving up my mother's music box.

Tears fell on my clenched hands, and I furiously brushed them away.

Hank shot me a look but didn't speak.

When we arrived at the house, I vaulted from the car and stormed inside. I was almost to the stairs when Joanne entered the foyer. "Lillian? Is everything okay?"

"Fine," I muttered, not slowing until I was in the haven of my bedroom.

Sinking to the bed, I released the sobs tearing at my chest.

I didn't know how long I sat there, spent, my heart aching with sadness. Would I be forced to return my only precious possession? Could Heather actually be that spiteful?

A knock at the door made me release a heavy sigh. No doubt Joanne checking up on me. *Now* the woman decided to show an interest.

Dragging myself from the bed, I opened the door, then gaped in surprise at Clinton.

I swiped at my cheeks, but the tears had long since dried. My eyes were no doubt red and puffy, mascara smeared down my face.

"Lillian, are you okay?"

The gentleness in his voice threw me off kilter. I drew in a shaky breath. "I'm fine. I just want to be alone."

"It's obvious something's wrong. Want to tell me about it?"

"Nothing's wrong."

"Not even this?" He held out the letter I'd abandoned in Hank's car. For such a close-mouthed person, the man certainly hadn't wasted any time spilling his guts.

"You read my mail."

"Do you have the music box?"

I sighed, looking down at my feet. "Yes."

"Why did you take it?"

I lifted my head. "It's mine. Or should be. It belonged to my mother. My father gave it to her on their tenth anniversary. My witch of a stepmother took everything else. She has no right to take that from me."

He lifted a hand and touched my cheek. "It means that much to you?"

His hazel eyes held a hint of compassion that threatened to release another flood of tears. I had to look away. "Please. I'd like to be alone."

He held out a hand. "Come with me."

"I told you, I—"

"Come on."

I didn't take his hand, didn't budge. "I'm

exhausted. I'd like to be alone."

"Want me to beg? Get down on my knees?" He quirked his mouth in a grin. "You'd like that, wouldn't you?"

A reluctant smile broke through. "I wouldn't hate it."

He laughed. "Trust me." He took my hand and tugged. I followed obediently while he led me down the stairs and to his study. "Have a seat."

I sat, and he opened a drawer in his desk, retrieving a small stack of stapled papers. He slid them across to me. "Fill this out for me."

I looked down at the sheaf of papers. "What is it?"

"An intake sheet. I'll need to know the details of your claim so I can represent you."

My head rose, and I stared at him incredulously. "You're going to take my case?"

His warm smile took my breath away. "I'll have to apply for *Pro Hac Vice* in order to practice in Ohio, but that shouldn't be a problem. I wouldn't trust something this important to any other attorney."

I was speechless with gratitude. When I found my voice, I said, "Thank you. I can't tell you what this means to me."

He tilted his head in a nod. "Now, in addition to the information on the forms, I'll need you to tell me exactly what happened." Holding a pen poised above a legal pad, he waited.

I settled back in my chair. "My stepmother never liked me. She knew I didn't like her, that I suspected she only married my father for his money. After he was diagnosed with cancer, she took care of him, playing the doting wife up to the end."

I fell silent, lost in the memories. She'd limited my visits. Claiming my father needed his rest. As if a visit from his daughter would cause harm. I'd barely seen him in those last days. Barely had a chance to say goodbye.

"Go on."

Clinton's gentle prod brought me back to the present. I twisted my hands in my lap, searching my mind for the correct way to convey what she'd done. Why it was so wrong. Sharing the story was difficult, but somewhat cathartic. My chest felt lighter as I continued. "I didn't know until after his death that she'd convinced him to change his will. To cut out the support for my tuition." I swallowed back another bout of tears. "It was my mother's dream that I finish college. Become a therapist, something I'd wanted since I was a small child. After the funds for my education were taken away, I couldn't afford to stay in school."

His expression was sympathetic, but he spoke in a business-like tone. "I'll need to see the will. Speak with the attorney who handled the probate. I'll do whatever I can to ensure you get what's rightly yours."

"I appreciate it more than you could know. I'll pay you whatever it costs."

He shrugged. "It's been a while since I've taken a case pro bono. That doesn't look good for my reputation."

Overwhelmed, I rose to my feet and came around the desk. He stood. I went into his arms, hugging him tightly. "Thank you," I whispered.

He squeezed back, then set me from him. "You can thank me when I win. Return those forms to me as soon as you can. Goodnight, Lillian. Get some rest."

Clutching the papers in my hand, I left the study, guilt at my earlier suspicions weighing heavily in my chest.

A small voice reminded me that just because he apparently had a penchant for rescuing damsels in distress, didn't mean he hadn't lost his temper and killed one.

****

The next morning before the session with Drew, I went to Clinton's study to give him the paperwork. I knocked, but he didn't respond. I tried the door, surprised when the knob turned under my hand. Even though Clinton didn't want anyone snooping around in his client files, he obviously trusted that his orders would be followed, and those who entered wouldn't pry into confidential information.

I placed the papers on his desk, then hesitated, wondering if he'd be angry that I entered his study without permission. I briefly considered. It felt dishonest to pretend I hadn't been in here. I'd take my chances on his ire. I left them and made my way upstairs for the session with Drew.

Drew lounged on the sofa in the sitting room, greeting me with a smile—a genuine smile, not a lecherous one. His upbeat mood was a nice change. He seemed to be more level, more relaxed than normal. I wanted to think I had something to do with it, but it was more likely the medication his physician had him on.

Whatever the reason, Drew's progress was a good sign. With my stepmother's handling of my father's affairs being looked into, and Drew improving, I could complete my doctorate, just as my parents dreamed.

Leave Shoal Harbor. Leave Clinton...

I shook off the despondency those thoughts brought. That had been my plan all along. There was nothing for me here.

That night, I was preparing for bed when a loud crack of thunder vibrated through the room. I rushed to the window, dread pounding through me at the sight of the darkening sky. Drops of rain shimmered on the glass, and a startling bolt of lightning illuminated the lighthouse. Something flashed in the top window of the tower, and I squinted through the darkness. Had that been a face? That was impossible. The weather was making me imagine things. Another enormous clap of thunder boomed, and I jumped back, dropping the curtain.

I shivered. *Stop this. It's only a storm. You're inside. You're safe.* I made a concentrated effort to stop the trembles running through my body. Choosing a book from the nightstand, I settled in bed to read. No way would I be able to sleep until the storm subsided. I tried to focus on the novel, but the words might as well have been written in Swahili for all I understood.

My mind kept wandering to the weather raging outside. With a determined effort, I focused on the page I'd already read no less than five times.

A particularly horrendous blast of thunder roared, then the lights went out, and I was plunged into darkness.

I froze, my legs quaking so badly, I couldn't climb from the bed. But then again, did I want to? Wasn't this the safest place to be?

I tried to remember if I'd seen any candles in the bedroom but couldn't recall. The storm was frightening enough, but a power outage was terror inducing. The only illumination was the occasional flashes of lightening across the draperies, which only intensified my fear.

Forcing my legs to work, I threw off the covers and stood. There had to be a candle in here somewhere. I was halfway across the bedroom floor, making my way through the dark toward the dresser, when a violent rattle shook the doorknob.

Chapter Eight

A scream left my throat. I couldn't think straight. Terror sent blood rushing through my eardrums, and it was several moments before I recognized Clinton's voice. "Lillian? Are you all right?"

On shaking legs, I rushed to the door, mindless of the dark. I jerked it open and summoned all my willpower not to launch into Clinton's arms. In the faint glow of the flashlight he held, I could barely make out his silhouette, but just having another human in the vicinity eased my terror.

"The power's out," I said stupidly.

"I know. I'm sorry. There are candles in the bathroom."

"I didn't know where to look. And it was dark…" I shuddered. "Why are you here?"

"Drew mentioned your fear of storms. I wanted to make sure you were okay."

"Thank you."

"Let's get those candles." His touch landed on my arm, warm and comforting. He guided me to the bathroom where he released me and opened a cabinet. Several candles, some new, some already used were stacked neatly in place. He grabbed the nearest one. Resting the flashlight on the countertop, he reached into his pocket. Flame from a lighter touched the candle's wick. He turned off the flashlight and slipped it in his back pocket. The flare wavered over his features, which were drawn into a look of concern I'd glimpsed only a few times.

"You're shivering," he murmured. He rubbed his hands up and down my arms. The friction of his touch sliding the silk gown along my flesh sent a skitter of desire over my spine.

I met his gaze in the candlelight. His eyes shimmered a golden green. We stared at one another for a few excruciatingly silent moments. He tugged lightly, and I was pulled against his chest. My bones turned to liquid, his touch leaving languorous heat in its wake. His hands slid upward, settling on my face.

"What am I doing?" He asked, his voice a tortured growl.

Before I had time to respond, he lowered his head and claimed my mouth. The kiss was gentle, his lips warm and coaxing. I opened to him with a small moan, linking my hands behind his neck. I pressed into him while a wave of undeniable yearning ached in my lower belly. *Madness. This is madness,* a voice whispered in my head. In spite of the truth in the words, I didn't stop.

"Lillian? Clinton?" At first, the origin of the words didn't register. I wondered how Clinton was able to speak with his mouth fused to mine. Then sanity returned.

Drew.

I broke the kiss and pushed away, wiping a hand along my mouth.

"God," he groaned, scraping a hand through his hair. He snatched up the candle, then brushed past me and out of the bathroom.

"In here, Drew."

I followed to find Drew standing in my bedroom, flashlight in hand.

"What's going on?" Drew looked from Clinton to me. "Are you okay?"

I smiled shakily. "I'm fine. Clinton found a candle."

He slowly nodded, his expression unreadable, but I sensed a hint of suspicion. None was revealed when he spoke. "Good. The storm's over."

I looked to the window. He was right. The storm had passed, and I hadn't been aware of it. Hadn't been aware of anything except Clinton and the desire his kiss had ignited.

Clinton moved across the room and placed the candle on my nightstand. "Let's go so she can rest. The power should be on soon. Hank is probably starting the generator now."

With that, they exited, leaving me alone with the flickering flame and the stirring embers of that unexpected kiss.

****

Clinton had been right. The power came on shortly after he and Drew left my room. Surprisingly, I was able to sleep and felt refreshed when I woke.

Later that afternoon, I was helping Joanne with the housework, trying not to think about the kiss. My efforts were futile. It was all I could think about.

While vacuuming the hallway that led to Clinton's study, an idea occurred to me. Joanne wasn't around to ask—she'd once again vanished unexpectedly—so I took it upon myself to make the call. I gathered furniture polish, dusting cloths, and window cleaner. Clinton hadn't been upset that I left the papers in his study. I wanted to do something nice for him to show my appreciation for his taking my case. If I didn't bother his client files, surely he wouldn't be angry that I was in his office.

I cleaned the windows and plaques, then dusted his desk. A locked file cabinet I hadn't noticed before stood in a corner. No wonder he didn't worry about keeping his door secured. Although he preferred no one enter his office, his client files were protected, so he didn't have to worry about confidentiality.

When I'd finished cleaning everything else, I rested my hands on my hips and scanned the large, full bookcase. To do a thorough job, I'd need to remove all the books. A task that would take at least a few hours. Sighing with resignation, I picked up a clean cloth. It wouldn't be much of a favor if I didn't have to work for it. Determination gave me a second wind, and I scooted an ottoman over to the shelf, standing on it so I could reach the books at the top.

Dusting only one shelf at a time to ensure replacing the books in their correct order, I worked methodically and steadily. In less than an hour, I'd finished half the shelves.

I glanced at the spine of the books, curious about the kind of reading Clinton Breckenridge did. Most of them were legal volumes, but there were also a handful of non-fiction books, and surprisingly, some novels. I smothered a small giggle. Clinton didn't seem the type of man who engaged in an activity just for entertainment.

I retrieved a book on bipolar disorder and sank to the ottoman. I thumbed through it, engrossed. I'd learned a bit about the condition while in school but had no idea of the many factors that contributed to episodes. I paid particular attention to the section on the role of environmental factors. Recent life events and interpersonal relationships were likely to incite episodes. No surprise there. Medication or no, Drew's failed romance and the tension with his brother no doubt had a dramatic effect on his state of mind.

I'd skimmed a few chapters and was about to replace it, making a mental note to ask Clinton if I could borrow it, when something slid from the pages to the floor.

I frowned, leaning over to search the carpet. I caught a flash of gold and reached down, picking a necklace up off the floor. A pendant dangled from the chain. The hair on my nape prickled, and cold tingles rushed over my skin. I rose to my feet, gaping in disbelief at the diamond heart resting in my palm. A diamond heart with an emerald in the center. Melanie's necklace. The one Drew gave her.

Why would Clinton have Melanie's necklace? And why would he hide it in a book?

The chain dangling from my hand was broken. As if in a violent scuffle. The scenario that occurred to me made my stomach cramp with nausea.

"Lillian?"

I whirled at the sound of Clinton's voice.

My heart pounded rapidly in my chest. I couldn't speak. Couldn't think of anything to say even if I'd been able to.

"What are you doing in here?" He lowered his brows. "You're pale. What's the matter?"

I shook my head slowly from side to side. I didn't try to hide the necklace. His eyes moved downward, then he raised his head to stare at me.

"Where did you get that?"

I finally found the ability to speak. "I was cleaning. It fell out of a book."

"You're not supposed to be in here."

"I thought—thought I'd clean for you. I'm sorry. I didn't mean to…" What was I doing? *I* was apologizing to *him*? "How did you get this necklace?"

His eyes narrowed. "Why? What do you know about the necklace?"

I pulled in a breath. "I know that Drew gave it to Melanie. That she never took it off. That you were the last person to see her alive."

"See her alive? You think she's dead?"

My heart weighted with sadness, I said, "The check wasn't cashed. No one's heard from her. And now…I find this."

"And you think I killed her." The words came out clipped, but his eyes held a touch of incredulity…or guilt?

I stared at him without speaking.

Grimness settled in his features. "Are you going to the police?"

Lifting my chin, I forced bravado into my tone. "Should I?" I wanted him to deny my accusation, to offer a plausible explanation. Anything other than the stony acceptance he conveyed.

"What do you think? You didn't answer my earlier question. Do you think I hurt her?"

"I—I don't know."

A muscle in his jaw ticked. He inclined his head in a terse nod. "Do whatever you'd like, but whatever you decide, I think it's time you left. I'll prepare your final paycheck. As soon as you can make arrangements, I want you gone."

Tears surfaced in my throat, but I swallowed them back. I was pretty sure he was a killer, yet I was hurt at being fired by him. My reaction made no sense. But then, nothing made any sense at the moment. How could he be a murderer after the kindness he'd shown? Why would he let me walk out of here when he knew I could go to the police? Why did it break my heart to learn he wasn't the man I thought he was?

****

An hour later, I was on the house phone with the airline. The first flight out to Cincinnati wasn't available until the next evening. I booked my flight and hung up, my head spinning with uncertainty.

I hadn't decided whether or not to contact the police about the necklace. Clinton didn't seem concerned. After considering, it occurred to me the discovery wouldn't necessarily prove anything. Not to the authorities.

But to me, it was obvious. Clinton and Melanie had struggled the day she disappeared. The necklace broke during the struggle. The reason Clinton had kept the jewelry was a mystery. Was it some kind of trophy? No. He wasn't a twisted psycho. He'd killed the woman to protect his brother. Not an excuse, but a reason. A motive.

Miserable, I left the house, walking aimlessly along the beach through a heavy fog. Evening had fallen, and with the sun's desertion, the night became chilly. I was barely aware of the cold as I trudged along the sand, ending up at the ledge where I'd escaped for daily solitude. If I ever needed solitude, I needed it now.

I climbed onto the rock and looked out over the water. What a disaster my endeavor here had been. I hadn't made enough money to continue my education. I hadn't helped Drew. If anything, I'd made things worse. And, to top it all off, I'd fallen for a man who turned out to be a killer. *Fallen for—as in love?*

I let out a wistful sigh. Not that it mattered how I felt. Aside from the whole probable killer issue, he certainly didn't appear to return those feelings, and even if he did—and he was innocent—what kind of future would we have? He'd never leave Shoal Harbor, and if I stayed, I couldn't finish school. Couldn't have the career I'd always dreamed of.

I laughed ruefully. I was working it out in my head like it was even a possibility. First and foremost, Clinton could barely stand the sight of me. Yes, he'd kissed me, but attraction was a far cry from love. A realization struck me. If he did love me, I'd give up everything. The lawsuit, my dream of a large, successful practice. I'd finish my education here. Settle for being a small town therapist and…

And what? None of that mattered. My time here was finished. Whether or not Clinton was guilty of Melanie's murder, it was over for us before it began. My accusations hung in the air like poisonous gas.

A breeze blew over me, and once more, I heard the cries. This time, much louder, more distinct. Human sounding.

I lifted my head and looked around. Peering through the mist, I spotted a figure hurrying along the shoreline. A woman's figure. For a moment, I was convinced it was the ghost, then I recognized Joanne's upright bearing and slight frame.

Where was she going in such a hurry at this time of evening?

I climbed from the ledge. Maybe now I'd find out what had been behind the housekeeper's unexplained absences.

Trying to keep enough distance that Joanne wouldn't spot me, I tracked her movements. She headed toward the peninsula where the lighthouse stood. When she rounded a bend, I hurried my steps, afraid I'd lose her.

On this stretch of shoreline, it was particularly dark. I was alone out here, other than Joanne. A woman I didn't know all that well. A woman who seemed to be up to something furtive. For a moment, I considered turning back.

No. There were too many unanswered questions surrounding this place, these people. Besides, it wasn't like I would be here much longer. I intended to get as many answers as I could before I left.

When Joanne opened the lighthouse door and disappeared inside, I rethought my decision. An abandoned lighthouse at night was pretty creepy under the best circumstances. Whatever the worst ones were, they couldn't be all that safe. But what was I afraid of? Joanne was a harmless old woman. She was on some kind of secret adventure, and I had a compelling urge to find out what that was.

I approached. Easing the door open, I cringed at the squeaking hinges. The interior was black, smelling strongly of must and mildew. Joanne was nowhere to be seen.

Feeling foolish and a little more than spooked, I backtracked to the door. No matter what Joanne was up to, it wasn't worth all this to find out. I put my hand on the knob and a small moan carried to me. I froze. Not a ghostly moan. A genuine, human sound. A woman in trouble. Maybe in pain.

It came from above. I released the knob and peered into the darkness, unable to make out a thing. Taking my phone from my pocket, I used the flashlight app to guide my way to the stairs.

Inching upward, I shone the light around. The stairs ended at a round cutout in the wooden platform. I stuck my head through, and a flash of movement caught in the glare.

I pulled myself onto the platform. Up here, the smell of mildew was overpowered by a sour odor like unwashed bodies. I glanced around and bewilderment made me halt. In the beam of the flashlight, I spotted a figure against the far wall. A woman.

I squinted, not believing my eyes. When I cast the beam lower, my suspicions were confirmed. Waves of shock and pity rocked me to the core. The woman's thin hands and feet were chained securely to a stovepipe attached to the wall. She wore a tattered blouse that might have once been white but was streaked with so much grime it was hard to tell. Tangled, filthy blond hair surrounded her pale face. She eyed me warily from sunken blue eyes rimmed with dark circles.

"It's okay," I said softly. "I'm here to help you."

I moved toward her, and she huddled tighter against the wall.

"Who are you?" Her words came out strangled, hoarse.

"My name is Lillian. I'm staying at Shoal Harbor.

What happened to you?"

She let out a low moan and shook her head. "So long. Been here so long."

"How? What happened to you?" I repeated.

She lifted her bound hands, as if in bemusement, then slumped lifelessly against the pipe.

I rushed to her side and knelt beside her, placing my fingers on her neck. She had a pulse, but it was weak. Her skin was stretched over protruding bones, like parchment paper on a skeleton. I had to get her out of here. Had to get help.

"Can you walk? We need to get you to a hospital."

She shook her head, tears squeezing from her closed lids. "No use. I'm a prisoner."

"Who are you? Who's keeping you here?" Even as I asked, I knew the answers to both those questions. The girl was Melanie Ross. And Joanne was her jailer.

Not waiting for her to respond, I searched the area, looking for a key. My hunt took several precious seconds, but I found one hanging on the wall across the room. Praying the key fit the lock on the chains, I snatched it up and rushed back to her side. My hands, slick with perspiration, shook so much I had trouble holding onto the key. Finally, I managed to secure my grip and slide it in. The lock turned, and she was free. *Thank God.* I took her frail arms gently in my hands. "Let's get you to your feet. I'll help you."

Where was Joanne? She'd come inside. But she wasn't in sight now. Maybe there was time.

Nodding, she let me help her to her feet. We'd taken half a dozen steps, me supporting her slight form, when a voice cut through the silence.

"That's far enough."

Chapter Nine

I whipped my head up. Joanne stood between us and the exit to the stairs.

"What's going on?" I demanded. "What have you done?"

Her face was haggard in the dim glow of a battery-powered lantern she held in her left hand. My heart sank when I spotted the small black gun she held in the other. "It's not what *I* did, it's what she did."

Melanie stiffened in my grip, her body trembling.

"Surely, you don't intend to keep her—"

"She was trying to ruin it all, the harlot. Her and that demon she was in cahoots with."

"Demon?" I mentally measured the distance from where we stood to the exit. Too far and with Joanne and her gun in between us, too insurmountable.

"She was ruining everything. Causing trouble between my boys. She and Sebastian Myers planned to blackmail Clinton. Sebastian put her up to getting in good with Andrew, then taking him for a fortune. I overheard it all."

I glanced at Melanie. Her chin angled toward her chest, and tears dripped down her cheeks. "I'm sorry. It was a mistake—"

Joanne cut her off. "The mistake was not killing you in the beginning. Trying to do the Christian thing and keep you alive. I should have known better." She shook her head. The shadows of the lighthouse accentuated the maniacal glint in her eyes. "After Mrs. Breckenridge, doing away with you should have been easy."

"Mrs. Breckenridge? Drew and Clinton's mother?" I said. "She committed suicide."

Joanne nodded. "After I fooled with her medication. I only meant for her to go back into the hospital. To leave me and the boys on our own. I had no idea she was spineless enough to kill herself."

My blood chilled. She'd screwed with a mentally ill woman's medication, triggered her suicide, and she called her victim spineless?

"You caused her to kill herself." I stared at her in disbelief. "Drew watched her do it."

She tsk-tsked. "That's my only regret. That poor Drew had to go through that."

She'd killed a woman, nearly killed another, and that was her only regret?

Melanie wrenched away from me with surprising strength and stumbled back to her wall. Joanne took a step toward her.

"Joanne." I held up my hands. "Please. Think about what you're doing. This is—" I almost said *crazy* but stopped myself. "Wrong. You can't go through with this."

"I had to do it. There was no other way."

"Okay. I get that." I kept my voice low, soothing. "But now we need to get help for her. Melanie is going to die if we don't."

Her lips trembled. "No other way."

"That's right. There's no other way to handle this. We need to get her to a hospital."

"Can't." She plodded slowly forward. "I knew it was all over when I saw you come in here. Time to put an end to this whole mess." Moonlight glinted on the shiny, deadly weapon.

I looked from Melanie to Joanne, who was eating up the space between them quickly. She muttered as she advanced. "I'll have to get rid of you both. Can't be running out here fetching for two. Trying to feed you both and take care of the house and the boys along with it. Not without anyone being the wiser. No other way."

"Joanne," I said firmly. She halted a foot from Melanie and swung her body toward me. "You can't do this. It's murder. You'll never get by with it."

Her face looked older suddenly, worn and ravaged. "I didn't want to kill anyone, but I don't have a choice now. It will fit right in with the legend. All the women who fall in love with the Breckenridges meet a tragic death."

I backed away and Joanne advanced toward me— no doubt realizing I should be first. Once I was out of the way, killing Melanie would be a breeze. She was half-dead already. She'd been out here for months, wasting away. At the mercy of a crazy woman. She'd more than paid for her crimes against Drew. If I could prevent it, she wouldn't pay with her life.

I kept backing, looking out the corners of my eyes for something—anything to use as a weapon. Nothing. There was nothing, and I was going to die.

A male shout bellowed from below. "Lillian? Are you up there?"

Joanne froze. She whirled toward the staircase, and I dove into her, knocking her to the ground. The gun skittered across the wooden floor with a sound that was both terrifying and beautiful at the same time.

Joanne flailed beneath me, reaching up wildly, her nails digging into my cheek. Sharp pain, followed by wet stickiness rendered me immobile long enough for Joanne to squirm from my grasp.

We both scrambled for the gun. Heavy footsteps pounded up the stairs. I reached the gun before Joanne did, snatching it up and rising to my feet. I pointed it at her head as she knelt on all fours.

"Don't move," I commanded, my voice trembling with tears.

"Lily? What the hell's going on?" Clinton's shocked words penetrated my consciousness, but I kept my attention on Joanne. I didn't budge until I felt his comforting touch on my hand. He gently took the gun from my grip. "It's okay now," he whispered.

I threw myself against his chest. One arm went around me, the other pointing the gun at Joanne, who rose slowly to her feet.

"Clinton, thank God you're here." Her voice trembled as if in fear. "This woman was trying to—"

"Save it, Joanne," he barked.

Against his chest, I muttered, "She kidnapped Melanie. She would have killed us."

"I know, sweetheart. Everything's okay now. I've got you."

"How did you find us?"

He let out a long breath. "I came to look for you, to make sure you were okay. I spotted a glow in the window of lighthouse." He broke off. "Joanne's been acting—off—for quite some time." He pulled away and glanced to where Melanie lay huddled in the floor. "Dear God, I had no idea just how 'off.'"

His voice was filled with ragged pain. What I'd suffered now seemed insignificant. The woman he'd thought of as mother was a killer. My heart broke for him. And for me. I'd fallen in love with him, and now I'd have to say goodbye.

****

Clinton stayed with Melanie and Joanne while I ran, breathless, to the house. I had to call the police and an ambulance. My heart thumped loudly in the thick, foggy stillness. Reality still hadn't set in. Joanne had actually kept that poor woman all these months in the lighthouse. Unbelievable.

When I reached the grounds and spotted a man standing outside the gate, my stomach dropped. Sebastian. He'd been in on it all along, but I was sure he had no idea Melanie was alive. I needed to keep him here until the police arrived. But first things first. I had to call for help.

Hoping he'd still be outside when I returned, I hurried in and dialed 9-1-1. Drew was nowhere in sight. Good. I didn't have time for explanations. I hung up the phone, then rushed back outside.

I headed to where Sebastian stood. This time he wasn't alone. Drew was with him, gesturing angrily, the two men facing off with no more than a foot separating them.

When I approached, Sebastian was saying, "You killed her. You or your brother. Stop lying." He grabbed Drew's shirtfront. "Tell me what you did."

Instead of answering, Drew pulled back his fist and punched Sebastian in the mouth. Sebastian grabbed his face and stumbled back, then launched toward Drew.

"Stop it!" I yelled. "Both of you stop it, right now."

They turned to look at me, both breathing heavily, both wearing a look of surprise that told me they hadn't known I was there.

"Lily?" Drew scowled. "This is between me and him. Let me handle it."

Sebastian still held one hand over his face. Blood dripped through his fingers. He staggered toward Drew, but I stepped between them. "Enough. Please. Just stop."

Sebastian glowered down at me. "Out of the way, Lily. He's had this coming for a long time."

I didn't remind Sebastian that he'd already taken the first punch, and he was likely no match for the younger, more muscular Drew.

"You want a piece of me?" Drew said from behind me. "Let's go, Myers."

I faced Drew to admonish him, but before I spoke, he did, eyes narrowed as he focused on me. "What happened to your face?"

I reached up and touched blood. I'd almost forgotten about my cheek. "It was—an accident. I—"

The sound of sirens cut through the night. In the distance, an ambulance sped toward the peninsula where the lighthouse stood.

"What's going on?" Sebastian demanded. He wiped his mouth, his eyes leveled on Drew.

I hesitated, wondering how much to reveal. "It's…someone is hurt."

"Someone who?" Drew took my upper arms. "Who's hurt, Lily? What's happening?"

"I—it's…" I didn't want to explain and take a chance on setting Sebastian off. Maybe he had a gun. After all, Joanne had one. Where were the police? I couldn't stall much longer.

A cruiser pulled up to the gate, but unlike the ambulance, its sirens were off. From the corner of my eye, I watched an officer climb from the driver's seat. Protection had arrived. It was time the truth came out, for everyone.

I tugged loose from Drew's hold and looked from him to Sebastian. "Melanie is…" I took in a deep breath. "She's alive."

"What are you talking about?" Sebastian said. "Where is she?"

"Lily?" Drew's face was pale in the light of the moon. "Is this true? How can it…what are you…" He shook his head vigorously as if clearing a nightmare.

The officer was approaching from behind Sebastian. Neither man seemed aware of his presence.

"You were in on it," I told Sebastian. "The two of you plotted to blackmail the Breckenridges. But when she disappeared, you thought it had gone bad and one of them had killed her."

Sebastian blinked a few times, then slowly shook his head. "No. It can't be. Are you telling the truth? Is she alive?"

I nodded. "She's not well. She's been kept prisoner at the lighthouse all these months. The ambulance is there for her."

"Miss?" The police officer had reached us by now. He was young, clean-shaven with the eager look of someone who wanted to please. "What's going on here? Have one of these men hurt you?"

Sebastian ignored him and advanced on me. "Who? Who kept her prisoner?" The words were bit out between clenched teeth. "Tell me what the hell happened, Lily." He'd reached me by now, and he took my shoulders in a painful grip.

"Hey there," the officer said. "Release her, sir."

"Tell me!" Sebastian screamed, ignoring the cop.

"Sir—"

Sebastian released my shoulders and grabbed my hair in a painful twist, pulling my face to his.

Drew dove into Sebastian, knocking him away from me just as the cop tugged handcuffs from his belt. Drew moved back and the officer slapped the cuffs on Sebastian's wrists and hauled him to his feet.

Drew came over to me and took me in a hug, soothing his hand gently along my hair. "Are you okay?" He whispered.

"Yes." I pulled away. "Thank you."

"Is she really alive?" At my nod, he said, "What in God's name happened? Who kept her prisoner?"

I looked into his face, knowing the vulnerability of his condition, but I couldn't lie to him. "It was Joanne."

"Oh my God." His voice broke, and he shook his head in bewilderment. "Why? How?"

"Joanne? The maid?" Sebastian still stood in the cop's grip. He moved toward me but the officer pulled him back. "What's going on? What's wrong with Melanie? Is she going to be okay?"

"You'll find out everything soon," I said to him, a part of me feeling pity even knowing his role in the blackmail. In spite of it all, he truly loved Melanie. Would I ever experience that kind of love?

****

By the time the police left, I was drained. The EMTs patched up the superficial wound on my face—a superficial wound that hurt like a mother.

Melanie had been taken to the hospital, Joanne and Sebastian, to jail. Clinton called for a report and was assured Melanie would survive.

My ferry was leaving in a few hours. There was no reason to try to sleep. Not enough time, and there was no way I'd be able to, not after the events of the past twelve hours.

I showered and packed. When I left my room, I found Clinton standing at the top of the stairs. "You're leaving?" His face revealed no expression, but his voice was weary, deflated.

"I am."

He nodded. "I'll pass over your case to a colleague who lives in the Cincinnati area. You'll be in good hands. He owes me, so you won't be charged."

A stone settled in my chest, so heavy my heart ached until I thought it would explode. I forced words around the knot in my throat. "Thank you."

"You're welcome." He picked up my suitcases and turned to the stairs.

"Clinton?"

He looked back at me, his brows raised expectantly.

"I'm sorry," I choked out. "About Joanne. I know you cared for her."

"It's okay. I've just got to learn not to trust people. Even those I love." He gave a bitter smile.

"I trust *you*."

Pain shadowed his features. "You thought I was a killer."

"I didn't know what to believe. The necklace…"

"When I gave Melanie the check that day, she ripped the necklace off and threw it at me. She told me to give it to Drew and tell him she didn't need his baubles."

"You hid it in a book."

He let out a heavy sigh and set the suitcases down. "I was trying to decide whether I should give it to Drew. I didn't want to hurt him, but I didn't feel right keeping it from him. I would take it out and look at it from time to time, wrestling with my conscience. The last time I had it out, I was reading that book. Drew came to my study door—" His head rose and a small smile touched his mouth. "It was the day you arrived. He came in to plead your case. To convince me to hire you. I shoved the necklace in the book and didn't think any more about it until I walked in and saw you holding it."

I slowly nodded, slightly ashamed of my interpretation of the innocent event. "You should have told me."

He shrugged. "I could see you'd made up your mind. I wasn't going to beg you to change it."

I let out a humorless laugh. "That brusque exterior you developed. It keeps people at arm's length. Keeps you from getting hurt."

He narrowed his eyes. "Are you psychoanalyzing me again?"

"I'm just trying to…" I lifted my arms, let them fall to my sides. Sniffing back tears, I rubbed my eyes. I was so tired. So empty and exhausted. I opened my mouth to speak, and a sob caught in my throat. I looked up at him. "Trying to keep you talking to me. *With* me. I know once I'm gone, I'll never see you again."

"And that would be bad because?"

I shrugged and shook my head.

"Tell me why it would be bad." He moved closer.

"Because, I…" I fell silent.

"Say it."

"Say what? What do you want to hear?" I searched his face.

"Say you love me," he said softly.

How much more pain was I supposed to take? But did it really matter? In a few hours, I'd be gone. This would someday be a distant memory. One that no longer had the power to cause such pain.

Someday a long, long time from now.

My shoulders slumping in defeat, I nodded. "Yes. I love you. I don't know how, I don't know when, but I fell in love with you."

I brushed past him and headed toward the stairs.

Clinton's voice stopped me. "Me too."

Squeezing my eyes shut, I halted. "You too what?" I whispered without turning around.

I didn't hear him move, but I sensed him behind me. So close, his breath shivered along the flesh of my neck. "I love you, too. Please don't go."

A cry left my throat, and I turned. He pulled me to him. His lips latched onto mine, and he rained kisses along my cheek, my jaw, my neck. "I love you, Lillian. But I know when it happened. The moment I laid eyes on you. I tried to fight it, but it was no use. The more I got to know you, your strength, your courage, the more I was sunk."

"Sunk?" I released a crying laugh. "Surely it's not all that dismal."

A deep chuckle rumbled through his chest. "I must be out of my mind to fall for a woman who wants such different things than I do."

I pulled away and stared into his face. "Like what?"

"Like success in the big city. A thriving practice. I can't leave Shoal Harbor, and you won't find those things here."

"None of that seems as important as it once did."

"Why is that?"

"Because I don't want to leave you. Success would be hollow without you in my life."

He smiled and brushed a lock of hair from my face, leaving his hand to rest on my cheek. "You need to finish school. We'll figure out a way to make that happen. I'll be waiting here when you do."

I briefly closed my eyes, relishing the feel of his touch on my skin. "I'll come back. Find a position in Shoal Harbor. I always wanted to treat a drove of patients, to have my name in psychology magazines. Working with Drew, I realized what matters more is truly helping the people I treat, not the number of patients I see or the accolades that come with a large practice. That's not what I need anymore." Stroking my fingers along his whisker-roughened jaw, I smiled through my tears. "I've found all I could ever want, right here with you."

Haunting at Spook Light Inn

Chapter One

I peered through the snow-dusted windshield at the large house looming in the evening dusk, and an unwarranted shiver of foreboding washed over my flesh.

From behind the wheel, my driver, Rita, made a sound that was somewhere between a squeak of trepidation and a sigh of admiration. "It's huge. And gorgeous, but kind of creepy, don't you think?" Her eyes were big and round behind the lenses of her black cat-eye frames.

"It is indeed." The sprawling structure was a combination of Southern plantation and Greek revival architecture; painted white and trimmed in a darker colored molding—perhaps forest green. The exact color was difficult to make out in the descending dusk. Narrow, darkened floor-to-ceiling windows peeked from between a portico of six Doric columns. Hanging by chains above the porch, a wooden board flapped in the icy wind. *Spook Light Bed and Breakfast.* The sign should have been welcoming, yet apprehension clawed at my heart.

Might as well get over that silliness. This would be my home for the next two weeks while I learned all I could about the Hornet Spook Light. The phenomenon, also known as the Tri-State Spook Light, Joplin Spook Light, Devil's Jack-O-Lantern, and a few other nicknames, had supposedly been spotted multiple times over the last few centuries in this area, at the border of Oklahoma, Missouri, and Kansas. I was here to do research for my book—*The Myth of Otherworldly Occurrences*. I chuckled and rolled my eyes. The only thing *otherworldly* about this place was its location thousands of miles from my warm, sunny home in Florida.

I glanced at Rita. Frizzy hair surrounded an oval face that seemed to have paled further since we arrived at the mansion. "Thank you for the ride. It was nice getting to know you." My publisher had sent Rita to pick me up at the airport in Joplin and drive me to my destination in Quapaw, Oklahoma. She was friendly and chatty, and the forty-five minute trip had flown by quickly. I looked back out the window at the imposing structure. Maybe it had flown by a little too quickly.

I reached for the door handle, but hesitated, filled with an odd reluctance. I wanted to stay within the warm confines of the SUV, say to heck with the book, return the advance I'd received, and forget I'd ever been to the area known as Devil's Promenade.

But, writing paid the bills. I needed to suck it up and get on with it. Besides, the last place I wanted to be right now was home, at least until Valentine's Day— and the wedding—were over.

Rita squeezed my arm through my thick coat, bringing my attention back to her. "I enjoyed getting to know you too, Cami." She popped the back lift gate with the inside lever, letting in a blast of icy air. "I'll help with your luggage."

"No, I've got it. No sense in both of us freezing to death." I handed her a tip, slipped on my gloves, and then, bracing myself, opened the door. Cold wind buffeted me. I had to struggle to climb out of the car. Boots crunching over the snow, I hurried to the back and grabbed my rolling suitcase and overnight bag. I'd packed light. The website said laundry facilities were available, so I saw no point in lugging an entire two-week wardrobe.

Head down, I tromped through the snow, shivering even in my warm coat as I tugged my case along the path. Other than the dim light glowing from the porch and the three-quarter moon drifting in the inky sky, the evening throbbed with a blackness deeper than any I'd ever experienced. Murky silence pressed around me. I'd never heard such an absence of sound, never seen—no, *felt*—such darkness.

I was a few feet from the steps when the sound of a throaty bark, followed by a high-pitched keening broke the stillness. Before the noise abated, another identical howl rose.

My footsteps halted, my knees weakening. What was that? Dogs? Coyotes? A shudder raced over my spine. At home in Miami, I didn't encounter wild animals, other than the occasional feral cat. The thought of being in close proximity with dangerous wildlife was completely unexpected—and alarming. I glanced around at the nearby woods.

How close were the creatures? Close enough to lunge, knock me to the ground, sink their sharp teeth into my throat, gouge my flesh until blood spurted in a red torrent, draining my life as I screamed in agonized terror…?

I vigorously shook my head. *Stop it, Cami.* Geez. Where had that thought come from? For such a pragmatic person, I was certainly entertaining fanciful notions.

Shifting the strap of my purse and carryall higher on my shoulder, I ascended the stairs to the porch. I reached out a gloved hand for the brass knocker, but before I touched it, the door swung open.

An attractive middle-aged woman, blonde hair piled atop her head in a messy, yet somehow sophisticated bun, smiled warmly from inside the doorway. Behind her, dim lighting glowed in a foyer elegantly appointed in gold and ivory.

"You must be Camille Burditt. I'm Loretta Delgado, welcome to Spook Light Bed and Breakfast." She stepped back and extended a welcoming arm. "Please, come in, I'm sure you're frozen solid."

"Yes, thank you," I managed through chattering teeth.

I started to step forward and something cold— colder than the frigid February air—brushed along my nape beneath my snow-dampened hair. I gasped and whirled, looking back out into the night. A brief glow penetrated the snowy dusk, then was gone.

"Are you okay, dear?"

It took a moment to respond, but I nodded, attempting to make sense of what had just happened. Tremors vibrated through my stomach, and I swallowed a knot of fear. Was that the spook light? No, of course it wasn't. The house sat several yards back from the road where the light had been seen—well, where people *claimed* they'd seen it. Those alleged sightings had been between the hours of ten p.m. And sunrise. This was much too early. So, what had I seen? Not a ghost. Specters didn't exist, except in the imaginings of weak-minded people who needed something to believe in.

Nothing, that's what I'd seen. I was just exhausted and freaked out by the remote wildness of my surroundings. But I could have sworn…

Nothing, it was nothing.

I hurried across the threshold, breathing a sigh of relief when the heavy oak door shut out the blackness, the eerie sounds, and the spot where I'd witnessed the inexplicable glow that was positively, definitely and for certain, *not* a ghost.

Chapter Two

Loretta led me through a foyer decorated in gold, ivory and sapphire. The furniture appeared to be antique, though well-preserved. A welcome fire crackled in a large fireplace beneath an intricately carved ivory mantel.

"Leave your bags at the bottom of the staircase. Holt will take them to your room."

I obeyed and followed her to an office off the main sitting area. She plucked a guest book off the desk and extended it, along with a pen. "Your room is pre-paid, but I need you to sign in and fill out your address and phone number."

She waited as I scribbled the information. I handed the paper back to her, and she placed it on the desk, then motioned with her hand. "This way, please. I'll show you to your room."

My luggage had disappeared. Holt—whoever he might be—had come and gone quickly and silently.

"There are only two other guests," Loretta said over her shoulder as we ascended the staircase. "Jin and Roxanne Kang. They are here for Valentine's Day. We had others who canceled reservations due to the inclement weather."

The staircase banister was polished oak and gleamed in the muted light from overhanging chandeliers. The stairs were of the same wood with a runner of woven material in a subtle blue and ivory floral pattern set into the center.

"Jean is our cook and housekeeper." Loretta continued up the stairs. "She has your room made up. I trust you'll be comfortable. If not, we have other rooms you may choose from."

"I'm sure I'll be quite comfortable wherever you put me."

We stopped on the first landing. "Your room is on this floor, along with the Kangs' room. But you are far enough apart that you shouldn't bother one another."

I didn't intend to bother anyone, no matter how closely situated our rooms were, but I didn't share that reassurance with her.

Portraits lined the walls on either side of us, but I didn't have time to study them as Loretta kept at a somewhat sedate, but ever-moving pace. She stopped at a door situated at the end of the hall and opened it, remaining outside for me to precede her.

"Your room is the Miner's Lantern. All of the rooms are named after one of the spook light legends, but I hope you won't be put off by the name. The room itself is quite lovely."

One of the legends claimed that the mysterious light was the lantern of a miner who was searching for his head after being decapitated in a mining accident. Another version was that an Indian Chief had been decapitated and was searching for *his* head. Either way, it was a creepy thing to name a room. But then, that was why I'd chosen Spook Light Bed and Breakfast, for the proximity to the Hornet Spook Light and the creep factor.

I stepped inside, and my breath caught in a gasp at

the beauty displayed before me. A large brass bed adorned with a mint green and ivory lace coverlet stood in the center of the room. Against one wall was a sleek walnut-stained, barre-front dresser, and a matching nightstand sat next to the bed. An ornate brass settee upholstered in the same mint and ivory was draped with what looked to be a handcrafted lace throw. Upon the dresser and small tables were a decorative miniature birdcage, a brass water pitcher and bowl, and repurposed painted bottles holding fresh flowers. The only blight on the gorgeous décor was a ceramic statue that sat on a side table of a headless man—the miner I assumed—holding a lantern.

"It's absolutely magnificent." My luggage sat on the gleaming hardwood floor amongst the delicate, woven rugs, and I almost felt like I was desecrating holy ground.

"I'm so glad you like it."

"It's perfect, thank you." The price had been a little more than I would have liked to pay, but my publisher was covering half. Now, seeing the room, I felt we had underpaid.

"The bathroom on this floor is shared by the other lodgers. If it is occupied and you wish to use the restroom on the next floor, feel free. However, the third floor is for staff only, so please do not wander past the second floor."

"I won't," I assured her.

"Cell service is intermittent, if not non-existent. You may use the phone on the nightstand." She pointed at a cream-colored vintage candlestick phone. "Although it doesn't get an outside line. It only reaches the office. Feel free to call if you need anything. Should you need to place an outside call, and your cell phone is not working, you may use the phone in the office or the library."

Should I need to make an outside call? In two weeks, I imagined I would need to make quite a few outside calls.

"Got it. Thank you."

"Declan Rush owns the bed and breakfast. He resides in the east wing of the ground floor and mostly keeps to himself. He leaves it to me to handle the needs of the guests. You will meet him but will not have much contact with him. It's very important that you allow him his privacy." Her mouth tightened in disapproval, as if I'd already committed the unthinkable and disturbed the sainted master of the manor.

"Of course, I'll not bother him."

"Good. I'll leave you to settle in. Dinner is at eight. Mr. Rush will be joining us. He does so on the first night of new guests' stay."

How benevolent of him, I almost said, but wisely refrained from doing so.

After Loretta left, I explored the room. I crossed the floor to an alcove inset with a small bay window where sheer mint green curtains were tied back. Beneath was a white sun-blocking drapery. Outside, snow drifted down into a soft blanket on the ground. It was so quiet. Such a change in pace from my apartment situated on a busy highway in downtown Miami. I would definitely be able to work here. What an awesome setting to write about the supernatural.

I wanted to revel in the peacefulness, but a niggle of discomfort at being out of my element prevented me from doing so. The whine of an eerie wind rose, and branches from a tree just outside the window slapped against the glass. I shivered, and my heartbeat accelerated. This winter weather would take some getting used to.

I unpacked quickly and pulled out my laptop. Settling into the alcove, I placed my computer on my lap and leaned back into the plush upholstery. I'd written for half an hour when my stomach growled. I checked the time. Seven. Another hour until dinner. Why did they eat so late?

I looked out the window again and found myself peering into the darkness, searching for the…thing I'd seen, whatever it was. A part of me was certain it was my imagination, while another part of me wondered if there was more to the eerie vibe of the spook light than I wished to believe.

****

Half an hour later, I'd finished laying out most of the groundwork for the book, going over my notes about the legends I'd already researched. I had to admit, they were quite intriguing. And, while I didn't believe some ghostly light bobbed and bounced on the road, I did wonder about the source. There had been too many sightings, too many photos to discount it completely.

Skeptics claimed it was car lights from Route 66. But supposedly, the legends had begun during the Trail of Tears in 1838—well before there were cars on the road—when a young Indian girl spotted the light moving through the trees. In 1946, the Army Corps of Engineers had come to check out the light and their analysis was that it was "a mysterious light of unknown origin," If even they couldn't attribute it to headlights, then I had to assume that wasn't where the light came from. Certainly, some of the sightings could be car headlights, but most likely not all of them.

Several paranormal investigators had studied it over the years. Many of them claimed to have seen it, and none could determine exactly what it was. The first documented report was in 1881. So, plenty of fodder for all the supernatural enthusiasts. But, what was the actual truth? That was what I was here to learn.

I stood and stretched. The time on my phone showed seven-thirty. Barely time to dress for dinner. And, with the master himself deigning to join us, I assumed it would be expected that we 'dress' for the evening meal.

I wanted to call my editor, Jillian, but I'd have to save that for another time. She'd want to know if I'd gotten settled in and how far along I was on the book. I'd tried to buy more time by playing the broken heart card, but she hadn't bought it. While she knew my heart was broken, she didn't have one, so she didn't care. Actually, that was unfair. Jillian had become a good friend. She just didn't have any patience for weakness or sentiment. And, pining over a fiancé who had jilted me for my sister came under the heading of sentiment. A lump rose to my throat, and I swallowed it back, blinking away the threat of tears. *I will not cry for you, asshole.* At least, not anymore. Though Lance had broken my heart, my sister's betrayal hurt the most. While Kathleen and I were as different as winter and summer, we loved each other. Or, at least I thought we did. Until the day—

No, I wouldn't think about it. Wouldn't dwell on the mess I'd left in Florida. I was here to focus on the book, and that was what I would do.

Chapter Three

I hurried down the hall for a quick shower, relieved the bathroom was empty but disappointed that I wouldn't have time to relax and enjoy the 1900's style bath—an odd mix of modern and historic with its black and white ceramic tile, double chrome mounted sinks with black lacquer framed mirrors, complete with a towel warmer.

I donned a knee-length midnight blue dress with a sheer high neckline gathered with a string of fabric that circled my neck to tie at back and a wide waistband leading into an A-line skirt. I left my hair loose, mainly because I had no time to do anything else. A quick swipe of lip-gloss and eyeliner were all the makeup I took time for.

I traversed the multitude of stairs to the bottom floor and realized Loretta hadn't shown me where we'd be having dinner. I listened for sounds that would guide me, but the house was as silent as a grave. Grave? Why would that word come to mind? Perhaps due to the legends of death surrounding the spook light and the sinister vibe I'd gotten since I'd arrived.

A shaft of light beneath a door off the main living area caught my attention. I went to the door and lifted my hand to knock. Before I could, the door swung open. A tall, glowering man with dark blonde hair and facial stubble that was just short of a beard stared down at me.

Startled, I brought my hand to my heart. "You must be Declan Rush," I blurted.

Neither confirming nor denying my guess, he said—with barely concealed irritation, "May I help you?" His deep voice held a trace of an Oklahoma accent.

"I'm Camille Burditt, I checked in this evening, and Loretta said dinner was at eight. I was just…"

His eyes were light silver, glittering like steel in the dim lighting. I couldn't continue with the intense stare trained on me. I swallowed.

"Yes, dinner is in the *dining* room."

I bit back my own irritation. "I assumed as much, but I do not know where the *dining* room is located."

"Down the hall. I was just going there myself. I'll take you."

"Thank you."

Barely keeping pace with his long strides, I followed him to an open doorway where I could now hear sounds of other people—the murmur of voices, the tinkling of glassware as I assumed the table was being set.

Declan Rush managed to avoid complete rudeness by pausing at the doorway and gesturing for me to precede him, which I did.

An attractive Asian man and a woman with vivid red hair and a curvy body poured into a form-fitting green dress stood speaking with Loretta. Loretta smiled warmly at Declan Rush and less warmly at me, although the smile was polite. "Camille, let me introduce you. Meet Jin Kang and his wife, Roxanne."

I shook their hands in turn, and we exchanged

pleasantries. Like Declan Rush, Jin wore a suit and tie, although his was not the same expensive cut. Nor did his body beneath it give the illusion of a sleek mountain cat trapped and ready to break free at any moment.

A woman who appeared to be in her early sixties with graying hair and wire-framed glasses carried a tray of champagne. The others already had glasses in hand. Declan and I each took a flute from the tray, and I offered the woman a smile.

"Thank you, Jean," Declan said.

"Welcome, Mr. Rush. Dinner will be ready in five."

"Fine, thank you." He said to everyone in the room, "Let's go ahead and take our seats."

Declan sat at the head of the table, the couple on his right, Loretta on his left. I settled beside Loretta.

"I'm so glad you could brave this weather to join us," Declan said, favoring us all with a glance. Whether he meant it or not, I wasn't sure, but it was a polite and hospitable thing to say. "Have you been to this part of the country before?"

"We haven't," Roxanne said. "We live in Arizona. We heard about this place and were fascinated."

"I was concerned when I saw the blizzard warnings," Jin put in. He placed a hand over his wife's. "But this is where my sweetheart wanted to celebrate our first anniversary, and I wasn't going to let weather ruin that for her."

Her face glowed with happiness as she leaned over and kissed him.

I forced a smile while my gut churned with nausea. Seriously? Was anyone really that happy? *You thought you and Lance were*, a little voice inside my head irritatingly reminded me. *Yeah, well, you see how that turned out.*

I jerked my head up in a moment of panic as I wondered if I'd said the words aloud. All eyes were on me. Had I?

"Ms. Burditt?" Declan stared at me curiously, making me think it wasn't the first time he'd spoken to me. "Have you been to Oklahoma before now?"

My face heated at the same moment relief swept through me. I hadn't spoken aloud. "No, no I haven't. I'm from Miami." Then I remembered the nearby town of the same name. "Miami, Florida, not Oklahoma," I added hastily, and unnecessarily, since I'd just told them I had never been to Oklahoma.

"Miam-*a*," Declan said.

"I beg your pardon?"

"The Miami in Oklahoma is pronounced with an 'a' sound at the end."

I frowned. "Oh, well, that makes no sense."

A small grin appeared on his full mouth. "Yes, well, what are you going to do?"

I smiled back. "Right?"

Conversation rose around the table about Oklahoma weather and how this wasn't typical, but they usually experienced maybe one or two blizzards a year. This one just happened to fall during our visits. "The worst thing for us about this kind of weather is the ice." Declan pushed his plate back and picked up his champagne. "It can often cause problems with power lines and roof cave-ins. If we happen to lose power, we do have a backup generator."

"What's the deal with the spook light?" Roxanne asked. "Do you think we'll be able to see it while we're here?"

Jin laughed. "Now, sweetheart, I told you, that's just a bunch of nonsense."

"I don't know." Declan's voice lowered into an almost hypnotic tone. "There have been many sightings and many unexplained happenings over the years. Who are we to say whether or not it's real?"

"Exactly." Loretta took up the cause, which I was certain was just a ruse to stir up interest in the spook light. "I've seen it many times. And, I've heard the legends all my life. So far, no one has come up with a logical, scientific reason for the spook light's appearance. So..."

Silence fell. Roxanne's eyes were round, her face animated. Jin still looked skeptical, but said nothing further, perhaps out of politeness, which is the same reason I kept my mouth shut. Supernatural spook light indeed...strange occurrences. Did they think we were children? Or gullible, like Roxanne?

After a delicious dinner of prime rib and truffle mashed potatoes, with apple crisp and homemade ice cream for dessert, Declan stood. "Would anyone like coffee or a cocktail in the library?"

"Yes, that would be nice," I said, simply because I though it the well-mannered thing to say. In actuality, I was anxious to escape to my room. The overtly polite conversation from our host had an underlying reluctance that made me uncomfortable. It was obvious he was simply performing a duty. Loretta had said he would only join us when new guests arrived. Hopefully, those occurrences would be limited during my stay.

Jin and Roxanne declined, saying they were exhausted and would just retire to their room. A look passed between them that made me fidget in discomfort. I didn't believe exhaustion was the true reason for their not staying for a nightcap.

Now, I wished I hadn't agreed to stay. Myself, Declan, and Loretta? My discomfort increased. I didn't know if her feelings were romantic or not, but Loretta apparently adored Declan Rush, the way she fawned over him. Was there something between them? She was perhaps five years older than he, but she was an attractive woman. He was a bachelor sharing a home with a single woman—well, I assumed they were both single, no spouses or otherwise significant others had joined us for dinner. It would only make sense if they were romantically involved, or at least Master of the House and Inn Keeper with benefits.

An unpleasant sensation washed through me. Why it should bother me if they were involved, I didn't know. Maybe it was the unprofessionalism and sordidness of the whole thing. It wasn't because I had designs on him myself. While he was admittedly attractive, his personality and air of superiority were off-putting to say the least. Attraction had to be more than the physical, and from what I'd seen so far, Declan Rush had no other appealing attributes.

I joined them in the library. Conversation was stilted, but I was still glad I'd come. The room was gorgeous, just like the rest of the inn, but the books were what had my attention. I glimpsed the spines, and my heartbeat accelerated. *The Catcher in the Rye, That Summer in Paris, To Kill a Mockingbird, Gone with the Wind.* A treasure trove of classics, some I hadn't read in years, and some I'd never read. If I kept pace on the book I was writing, I might actually find some down time to read.

"Is the library open to guests?" I asked boldly. I didn't care if it was rude. I wasn't going to miss out on the opportunity to explore simply because I was reticent.

"Yes, of course." Loretta offered one of her professional and just short of genuine smiles I was beginning to recognize. "We encourage our guests to use the library. Help yourself to the books, relax here, you are free to work here, if you'd like, although I can't guarantee you'll have it all to yourself."

"I don't know, Jin and Roxanne don't seem like they're here to catch up on their reading."

The first authentic smile I'd seen spread across Declan's lips. "No, I don't believe that's their main interest."

Oddly, I felt like I'd scored some sort of victory. Eliciting a humorous smile from Declan Rush? I'd accomplished the impossible.

Always one to leave them wanting more, I said, "Thank you for a lovely evening, but I'm starting to feel the effects of my day of travel. If you don't mind, I believe I'll retire."

"Of course." Was that relief I heard in Declan's voice? He'd completed his duties and wouldn't be bothered with me further.

****

Once in my room, I settled into the alcove and wrote late into the night. The legends surrounding the spook light were so numerous, I barely made a dent.

When I could hold my eyes open no longer, I changed into an old, tattered black sleep shirt proclaiming "I Need Coffee" and settled into the massive bed. I sighed with delight. The mattress was so comfortable, I felt as though I'd landed in a vat of marshmallows.

Lying back on the oversized feather pillows, I opened a King book I'd been reading during my travels, wishing I'd snatched one of the classics from the library.

I was semi-engrossed in the story when a rattling sound made me jump. The wind had risen so fiercely, the window vibrated. Beneath that sound was another…the yowling of coyotes? I should have asked Loretta about the identity of the animals I'd heard. Not that it would make much of a difference, except, if it were coyotes instead of dogs, I would limit my outside wanderings to the immediate area around the house.

Another sound—almost like that of a human moan—rose. I yelped and slammed the book closed. Tossing it on the nightstand, I threw back the covers and climbed from the bed. Although not sure I wanted to identify the sound, I hurried to the window, the hardwood floor cold against my bare feet.

I rubbed my arms against the chill, then drew the curtain back and looked outside. Darkness pushed against the glass like a physical being. Snow and a sprinkling of stars made the night only slightly less black. What had I heard? Snow falling? No, that was ice pelting the window. I hadn't been around snow often, but I knew it didn't make that kind of sound.

A flash of something bright caught my attention. I pushed closer to the window, my nose practically touching the pane. There, in the corner of the yard next to a bare-branched shrub. A wisp of something…

I grabbed my cell phone and zoomed in. My heart

beat in triple time as I looked through the phone camera. A ghostly figure...no other way to describe it. The gauzy essence was in the shape of a person, undefined, yet unmistakable. A woman, it seemed— long hair flowing behind her, the skirt of a dress billowing around her legs.

She seemed to be staring up at the window...

She, ha, it was nothing, no 'she,' no ghost, just my imagination. That's what I got for reading Stephen King in a peculiar, spooky house in a strange place. Plus, I was just overtired from my trip. But, still, I was seeing it. Wasn't I? I squinted at the enlarged image through my cell. Yes, it was right there...

I punched the video option on my phone and hit 'record.' I would study it further. Figure out if I was seeing what I thought I was seeing. And if I was, I could show others, so I would know I wasn't crazy.

I'd only been recording for a few seconds when the image just...floated away, dissipated somehow. Chills brushed over my flesh. I dropped my arm holding the phone and stared stupidly out the window. Frowning, I touched Play on the video. The screen filled with the view out my window, but the apparition was not there. What the...?

The shrub was in place, in the recording. Just where I'd seen the...thing, whatever it had been. But now, there was nothing.

I took a deep breath. I wasn't sure whether to be relieved or concerned. Whether I was seeing things, or if there really was a *thing.* Perhaps I truly was going crazy.

No...just overly tired, an overactive imagination and the masterful conjurings of Stephen King.

I slipped back in bed and tossed the book into the nightstand drawer, then shut it safely inside. I reached for the bedside lamp but paused before switching it off. Maybe it wouldn't hurt to leave a light burning. After all, I was in an unfamiliar place, and the bathroom was down the hall. If I needed to get up during the night, I'd have to be able to see.

Satisfied I was being practical, rather than frightened, I snuggled into the covers. But it was a long while before I fell asleep. My ears and eyes were trained on the window…my mind brimming with the strangeness of my experiences at the Spook Light Bed and Breakfast. And I'd yet to be here for twelve hours.

Chapter Four

I slept fitfully in spite of the comfortable bed. The next morning, I awoke groggy and annoyed with myself. Ghosts, *pshh*. If I weren't careful, I'd become one of those gullible sheep I targeted in my books. I showered and dressed in worn jeans and a ruby red mock-neck knitted sweater. I pulled my long hair back into a ponytail and decided not to bother with makeup.

It was eight, and I'd missed the communal breakfast at seven. No worries. I'd just as soon grab something and have a bite alone.

The maid from last night—Jean, Declan had called her—was in the kitchen, which was attached to an informal dining room. It was large with a marble center island and copper pots hanging from racks along the walls.

She smiled brightly. Her hair was tucked into a black hairnet, and a white apron spattered with food stains hung askew on her round frame.

"Good morning," she said in a heavy Oklahoma accent. "We weren't introduced last night, but I'm Jean Hibbert."

"I'm Camille Burditt. Cami."

"I was gonna ask how you slept, but judging by those dark circles, I'm guessin' not well." She wiped her hands on a towel hanging from her apron. "I've got just the thing." She opened the fridge and bent inside.

When she straightened, she held a cucumber and a small spray bottle. She sliced the cucumber, spritzed it with the liquid, and brought the slices to me. "Here, press these against your eyes."

"What are they? I mean, I know they're cucumbers, but what did you spray them with?"

"My secret remedy. Cucumber spritzed with rosewater. Here, go on."

I felt foolish but did as she suggested.

"Leave 'em for at least five minutes."

"Sure. Okay." It felt odd, disorienting to cover my eyes with the vegetable and plunge into complete darkness, while a woman I just met chattered endlessly as—judging from the sounds and smells—she busied herself making breakfast.

Minutes later, she said, "You can take 'em off."

I pulled the cucumbers away from my eyes, surprised that I felt less groggy. "So, how do I look? Bright-eyed and ready to conquer the world?"

She chuckled. "Let's start with getting breakfast in you, and we'll see where it goes from there."

She offered me a choice between a bagel, pastries, or a boiled egg and toast. I chose a bagel with flavored maple nut cream cheese. Somehow, it was tastier than the average bagel. Maybe it was because my body needed a treat after my unsettling experience last night.

"I hope you like it," Jean said. "I made a fresh batch this mornin'."

I swallowed and widened my eyes. "You made these? Homemade bagels?"

"Yep. Much better than the store bought kind."

"I'll say." So, that explained why it was like little bites of Heaven.

"So, where you from? You married? Boyfriend?"

I smiled at her prying questions. I liked her, and I didn't mind. "I'm from Miami, Florida. I recently got out of a relationship."

"I'm sorry. Breakups can be hard."

"Yes, they can." *Especially when your sister steals your fiancé.*

A newspaper—*Quapaw Daily*—lay beside my plate. I grinned. That wasn't something I saw much. A printed newspaper? How retro.

I picked it up and sipped my coffee as I perused the articles. A story on the inside page caught my interest. "Local Woman's Death Ruled an Accident." Why was it that *death* was always an attention-grabber?

The article stated that Eleanor Chaney had drowned in Spring River in August of last year. The police had investigated but found no evidence of foul play. There was no suicide note. The coroner's determination was that she'd gone farther out than she thought and became disoriented, unable to make it to the bank. It was at night, and the darkness added to her disorientation.

My insides tensed. Spring River was nearby...Rita and I had passed it on the way in. The woman had died not far from here. A death near the spook light? Surely I could work that into my book somehow. Not that I wanted to take advantage of the poor woman's misfortune, but it could tie in to the story. I could write about a modern death among all the old legends.

"Something catch your fancy?"

I started at Jean's voice. My hand that held the coffee cup shook. "Sorry to be so jumpy. No, just engrossed in the news." Should I ask her about the death? Maybe not just yet, not on my first morning. I didn't want to seem like a nosy reporter, or that I was pumping her for information. She most likely knew the woman. This was a small town. Most people in the area probably knew one another.

Jean took the decision out of my hands when she eyed the paper. She wiped tears from her eyes with her fingertips. "Poor dear. God rest her soul."

"Did you know her?"

"Yes of course. Eleanor Chaney. We were real close."

I looked back down at the paper. A photo of the woman accompanied the article. She was attractive, but her expression showed an unpleasant emotion—anger, disapproval? Without it, she would have been much prettier. "She drowned in Spring River," I said. "They said her body was found near Devil's Promenade? I thought this *area* was called Devil's Promenade."

"It is. But it's also the name of a bridge that goes over Spring River."

The name made the death...the whole thing...even worse, somehow. "So tragic."

"Yeah. They say it was an accident but ..." She heaved a deep breath. "I don't know. I wonder how that could be. She grew up swimmin' in that river. And I don't believe she'd go in the water alone, at night."

A quiver ran through me. "Do you think it was suicide? Murder?"

Jean lowered onto a chair next to me and picked up the newspaper. She ran a finger lovingly over the picture, a sad smile on her wrinkled face. "Eleanor was not one of the happiest people I've ever known, but she thought too much of herself to commit suicide. I don't buy that she'd take her own life."

"So you think someone killed her?"

"I don't know. The thought makes my skin crawl. This is a small town. Everyone knows each other. Eleanor wasn't exactly well loved. And, her family history caused some hard feelings around here, but I don't know anyone who hated her. Leastwise not enough to want her dead."

Was Jean right? Had the woman been murdered? Surely if that were true, there would have been evidence pointing to foul play. "Well, either way, accident, murder, or suicide, it's very sad."

"Yes. And poor Mr. Rush. He's beside himself."

"Mr. Rush? He knew her too?" Was she his girlfriend? Not his wife, their last names were different. But then, not all women took their husband's names…

"Knew her? Well, I'll say. She was his sister."

"Oh no…his sister. He must be heartbroken." Maybe that explained his foul mood. I felt bad about my spiteful thoughts. The guy had lost his sister six months ago. No wonder he wasn't exactly Mr. Sunshine.

"Yeah, he sure is. All the family he had. And our maintenance man, Holt, was her husband. The two of them ran the inn together, until Eleanor died."

"I'm sorry. What a tragedy."

Jean glanced around then leaned in as if to whisper a secret. "Tell me something, have you seen her…Eleanor's…spirit?"

I frowned. "Her spirit? No, of course I haven't. That's ridiculous."

"You don't believe in ghosts?"

I let out a scoffing laugh. "Of course not."

"Then why are you writin' a book about paranormal stuff?"

Word traveled fast at the inn. "It's to *disprove* the paranormal, not confirm it."

She gave a smug smile. "We'll see if you feel that way after you've been here a few days. I've seen Eleanor's ghost."

I stopped just short of saying she was out of her mind. But, she most definitely was. I opened my mouth to say something a bit more diplomatic, but clamped it shut when a creaking noise caught my ear. My eyes widened.

Jean laughed. "That ain't Eleanor, it's just this old house settling." She stood and brushed her hands down her apron. "When you meet Eleanor, you'll know it."

An involuntary shiver zipped over my flesh. Before I could reply, Jin and Roxanne entered the kitchen. They looked completely rested, although I would guess they had been kept up a good part of the night too— most decidedly for reasons other than mine. I tried not to let that notion unduly annoy me. I settled for being *duly* annoyed.

"What can I get you?" Jean rattled off the menu.

"I highly recommend the bagels," I offered. "They are *homemade*. Can you believe it?"

Roxanne's brows rose. "I don't think I've ever known anyone who made their own bagels. Sounds delicious. That's what I'll have."

Jin opted for pastries. They both had tea, and we chatted about non-essential topics and how long they'd stay. When I asked what they planned to do while here, they shared a not-so-secret grin, and it didn't take a Mensa member to interpret it.

Okay, we get it, you're in love, you can't keep your hands off one another. I grimaced at my uncharitable attitude but still, they were a little...sickening. Well, they'd only been married a year. Wait until the new wore off, and until one of them cheated. That would wipe those silly grins off their faces. I halted my train of thought. What was wrong with me? I'd never been so cynical. I was determined not to be now. I would not let my cheating no-good fiancé and my Judas sister turn me into a bitter old crone. Jin and Roxanne were perfectly adorable. I was glad to see they'd found happiness. Maybe it would last. What did I know?

In spite of my newfound supportiveness, it didn't mean I had to watch their displays of passion. I finished my bagel, and Jean refilled my cup.

I stood. "If you'll excuse me, I have work to do. I'll see you at lunch, perhaps?"

Roxanne smiled. "We'll be there."

"Great, see you then."

I took my coffee and meandered through the downstairs. I more closely studied the portraits we'd passed last night. Some were paintings and others were studio photographs. One was of a couple and two young children, a boy and girl. Perhaps Declan and his sister with their parents. I continued along, passing by those of unfamiliar people, but paused in front of one of Declan, along with Eleanor, who I recognized from the photo in the newspaper. Eleanor was lovely, but she didn't look happy in this picture either. Was she just a miserable woman? I focused on Declan. He was smiling, looking younger, boyish, carefree. His gray eyes were alight with mischief. He seemed much happier then, even though it was just a photo. What had happened to turn that boyish cheerfulness into acrimony?

My gaze was drawn to a necklace Eleanor wore—a silver chain with a charm in the shape of a key dangling from it. The key was inset with diamonds and black stones. Unique, and beautiful. I couldn't take my eyes off it. Had her husband given it to her? Someone had gone through a lot of expense and trouble to bestow such a gift on her. But from the expressions I had caught on the woman's face, she wasn't the type to appreciate kind gestures from people who cared about her. Had her unfeeling animosity driven someone to do the unthinkable? I was jumping to conclusions, but once it took hold, the thought wouldn't let go.

Chapter Five

Lunch was an uncomfortable event with only me and the happy couple in attendance. They couldn't keep their hands, or eyes, off one another. I left the table as soon as I could and decided to take a short, brisk walk to keep the calories from latching onto my frame, which had the tendency to carry extra pounds.

I bundled up in my coat and boots and stepped out into the cold. The icy wind immediately stole my breath. This would definitely be a short walk.

I tromped down the stairs and onto the walkway. Someone had been busy. Snow was piled on either side, and the path was littered with tiny white rocks that I assumed were salt. Good. Had the cement been covered in ice, I'd likely have fallen on my butt.

Tucking my hands in my pockets and turtling my head into the neck of my coat, I forged onward. I wasn't sure where I was going, but not far. I didn't relish tromping through two feet of snow.

I reached the end of the drive and looked up and down the road. The shoulders were fairly free of snow, due to protection by the overhang of trees. As I was deciding which direction to go, a low humming sound from behind caught my attention. I looked back to find a golf cart approaching. A man I didn't know sat behind the wheel.

He pulled up and stopped beside me. He lifted the

flap of plastic hanging down over the side and smiled. "Hey, is everything okay?" He was nice-looking, with dark hair and blue eyes and a dimple to the right of his mouth.

"Yes, sure. I was just taking a walk."

"Kind of cold for a walk." He stuck out a gloved hand. "I'm Troy Percival, groundskeeper for the Spook Light."

I shook his hand. "Camille Burditt, guest at the Spook Light."

"Come on, hop in. It's freezing out here."

"I was trying to get a little activity, walk off my lunch."

"Ha, bouncing around in this thing is exercise enough."

Since my skin was starting to sting from the cold, and my body felt like a block of ice, I made my decision and climbed in beside him. "Thank you."

"No problem. By the way, I don't know if Loretta told you, but the inn owns half a dozen of these carts, and guests are welcome to use them any time. I'll show you where they're kept."

He drove us along a path that circled to the side of the house and stopped in front of a freestanding garage with three separate doors. He stopped in front of the one on the right. "This is where the golf carts are kept. The code is 1906." He punched the keypad, and the door slid open. Inside were neatly lined up carts. He pulled in and we parked. "So, help yourself any time."

"Great. Thanks." We climbed from the cart and stepped outside. He lowered the door via the keypad and saluted. "Well, nice meeting you, Camille. I'll be around so if you need anything, give me a shout."

"Thank you, I will." I grinned. Troy's and Jean's friendliness was a balm that eased the sting of Loretta's phony, reserved politeness and Declan Rush's more overt frostiness. I now felt less unwelcome, less like an interloper and more like a guest. And Troy wasn't bad looking at all. My stay here might be more pleasant than anticipated.

****

After dinner that evening, I took my laptop down to the library to work on my book. A change of setting always helped stimulate my writing. Plus, I loved the library and had been itching to visit it again.

When I opened the door and stepped inside, I was greeted by the faint, lingering scent of cigars. Low music played—some type of instrumental. Nothing I was familiar with.

A man stood with his back to me, looking out the floor-to ceiling window into the snowy night. He turned, and my heart gave an odd, unexpected little flutter when I recognized Declan.

"I'm sorry. I didn't know anyone was in here. I wanted to work on my book."

He gestured with the glass he held toward the sofa. "Please, make yourself at home. I won't disturb you."

Hmmm. Not the reaction I expected. "Thank you." I nodded toward an old-fashioned phonograph where a record played—the source of the music.

"Where did you get that? I didn't think they had been around in decades."

"It belonged to my grandfather."

"It still works. Wow."

He smiled. "A little scratchy, but I think that's how these old records were meant to be listened to."

"Who is that?"

"Tommy Dorsey."

I cocked my head. "Mr. Rush, are you sure you're from this century?"

A grin tugged at his mouth. "Sometimes, I wonder that same thing."

"Listen, I was wondering…" I held the laptop to my chest and approached him. "Could I ask you some questions?"

"About?"

"I'd like to interview you regarding the spook light. For my book."

He frowned and took a sip from his glass. "I would rather not."

"Why not? It might bring in business for the bed and breakfast."

His frown turned into a scowl of irritation. "We get quite enough business as it is."

"At dinner, you mentioned that it's real. I thought that might mean you had stories surrounding it. That you might want to get the word out about it."

"I'm afraid you thought wrong. I was just making conversation." He finished off the contents in his glass and set it on the bar. "Now, I have work to do. If you'll excuse me."

"What kind of work?"

"I beg your pardon?"

"What kind of work do you do? Do you do something other than own the inn?"

"I'm an architect. I office out of my home. Will there be anything else?" He moved past me toward the door.

I was determined to get to the bottom of his

unreasonable attitude. I blurted, "Why don't you like me?"

He faced me, his jaw tight. "What makes you think I don't like you?"

"Because, you aren't friendly to me."

"Has it ever occurred to you that I don't know you, and I have no reason to be friendly to you? Loretta runs the inn. It's her job to keep guests happy, not mine. If you have a complaint, see her."

I grinned. "Do you think she'll resolve my complaint when I tell her it's you?"

He looked taken aback for a moment, then he smiled. "You're a bit impudent, aren't you, Ms. Burditt?"

"I suppose. And, please, call me Cami. This isn't the nineteenth century." Although, since my arrival, I almost felt like I'd stepped back in time. I wondered if he'd suggest I call him Declan, but I didn't think so. That would have been much too personal, too sociable.

"Thank you, but I don't anticipate we'll have the opportunity to get on a first name basis. I'm sure we won't see one another often."

Got it. Duly noted. In other words, stay out of my way.

"Yes, of course." I twisted my hands nervously. "I just learned what happened to your sister. I'm sorry."

He narrowed his eyes. "You *learned*? You've been digging around in my personal life?"

"No, no of course not."

I could feel tension building in him, like a volcano just before it erupts. "No? You aren't gathering material for your book?"

"Well, yes, I am. But that's not why I mentioned

your sister. I don't plan to include her in my book."

"Then what's your interest?"

I dropped onto the sofa and sat my laptop on the cushion beside me. I swept a hand through my hair. Geez. This man could *not* have a normal, polite conversation. "I just wanted to offer my sympathy. My book is about the falsehoods of paranormal happenings, so it would have nothing to do with—" I halted. "Wait…was there something…unusual about your sister's death?"

His face shuttered. "What happened to my sister is none of your business. Now, if you'll excuse me."

He circled around the desk and opened the door.

"I'm sorry. I didn't mean to upset you. I just thought it might help to talk about it."

"I don't need your help, Ms. Burditt. I don't even know you."

I lifted my chin and clamped my lips shut, fighting back the sudden urge to tear up. I didn't know him either, so why should his harsh words sting? It wasn't as though I even liked him. He was sooo rude. I had never met anyone so rude in my life. And, I was involved with the publishing world where making a buck was high priority over sparing people's feelings.

****

The next morning, I met Holt—the heretofore unseen hauler of my luggage. I'd asked Loretta about taxi service, and she offered the maintenance man-slash-bellhop as my driver for the day. Through the local librarian, I'd made an appointment to speak with some locals about the spook light.

A man—Holt, I assumed—was waiting in the foyer when I came downstairs. "Camille? Hi, I'm Holt

Chaney. Nice to meet you." He had a friendly, open face. His reddish-brown hair flopped over a wide forehead. He wore a flannel shirt and faded jeans. "I heard you need a ride."

"I do. Thank you."

He led me outside where a silver Mercedes sat running in the circle drive. He opened the passenger door, and I climbed in, grateful he had already warmed the car. I sighed in contentment as heat blasted the interior.

Holt pulled out onto the road and turned east. "I hear you're from Florida?"

"Yes, well, I'm from Kentucky. Moved to Florida when I was thirteen."

"Bet it's a whole different world from this place."

"Very different. If nothing else, much warmer."

He chuckled. "Yeah, for the most part, our winters are pretty mild, but we usually get a few good blizzards a year. The ice is the problem around here. Freezing on power lines, accumulating on roofs and causing cave-ins. It's a godawful mess sometimes."

I peered out my window where I could see almost nothing but white, with a few bare-branched trees scattered intermittently. "You think that will happen this time?" I couldn't imagine being in that huge, creepy house during a power outage. Or when the roof caved in. That could potentially kill someone, or at least cause severe injuries.

"It might, but not at the house. It's shored up pretty good. Well, you might get a power outage, but the roof is gonna hold. Me and Troy made sure of it."

"How many people are employed by the inn?"

"There's Loretta, me, Troy, Jean. And then Declan

hires a cleaning service to come in once a week to give the entire house a good once-over, and to clean rooms when we have several guests checking out. That way, Jean only has to worry about the cooking and light cleaning."

"You all do a wonderful job. It's a lovely place."

"Thank you. We try."

As insensitive as it seemed, I wanted to bring up Eleanor's death. Not to be nosy, but I wanted to offer my sympathy, even though it hadn't exactly been welcomed when I'd done so with Declan.

Maybe I'd better not. Definitely not in our first interaction. I'd be here for two weeks. Plenty of time to bring up his deceased wife.

Chapter Six

I yawned as we pulled into the parking lot of Anna's Donut Shop. Getting up at six a.m. Was a challenge. Too bad I wasn't meeting teenagers. They wouldn't have wanted to meet me at such an ungodly hour. I thanked Holt as I climbed from the car.

"You're welcome." He waved. "Just call the inn when you're ready to be picked up."

I nodded and shut the door.

Icy wind stung my cheeks as I rushed to the entrance. When I pulled the door open, bells jingled to announce my arrival, but no one looked up, not even the workers behind the counter. Apparently, they were all accustomed to the noise, which defeated the purpose of alerting them to customers.

The sugary scent of baked goods filled my nostrils, and I inhaled the fragrant aroma, along with the enticing scent of coffee that hung in the air. My stomach rumbled. How could I be hungry this early? I was barely awake.

Of the dozen white hard plastic tables, half were occupied. At one of them sat three elderly gentlemen. A man with thick white hair wearing a blue chambray shirt waved at me. These must be the locals I was scheduled to meet. I smiled and headed to the table. Another of the men—tall, slender, balding—stood and pulled out the empty chair.

"Thank you." I smiled at each of them and slid into the chair. "I'm Camille Burditt."

They introduced themselves; the man in the blue shirt was Fred, the one who'd pulled out my chair was Elbur, and the third was Wally. He was shorter than the others, plump, wearing denim overalls and a white thermal shirt.

I pulled my notepad out of my purse. "I appreciate you gentlemen meeting with me."

"Sure thing." Elbur wrapped age-spotted hands around his coffee cup. "Not much else to do this time-a year. Besides, always willing to help out a pretty girl. Although, how talking about the spook light can help you is beyond me."

"I'm writing a book. I'm working on a chapter dedicated to the spook light. I've done research, of course, but it's not the same as actually being here, actually visiting with people who have seen it."

"Before we get started," Wally said. "What can I get you? Anna makes the best donuts in North America."

"I'd love a cinnamon twist and a coffee."

He stood. "Coming right up." He held his finger out like a gun and pointed at each of his friends, then at me. "Don't say nothin' interestin' until I get back."

"Cross my heart." I made an X over my chest to prove my sincerity.

He returned in a few moments with a steaming cup and a donut that looked so delicious my mouth literally watered.

I took a bite of the twist and closed my eyes, barely suppressing a moan of ecstasy. "This is amazing."

Wally grinned as proudly as if he'd made it. "Told

you."

I sipped from my steaming cup of coffee and opened my notepad. "If it's okay, what I'd like to do first is get a little information from you about the legends."

"Reckon you researched them legends already didn't you?" Elbur asked.

"Well, yes, certainly. But I still want to hear your versions of them." I looked at Wally. "What about you, Wally? What have you heard over the years?"

"Well, there's a bunch. Some claim it's the spirits of a young Quapaw Indian couple. The girl—an Indian princess—fell in love with a brave. They were forbidden to marry 'cause he didn't have a huge dowry. They ran off together and her daddy—the chief—sent his warriors after her. They caught up to 'em at Spring River. The young couple held hands and plunged to their death in the river. They jumped off Lover's Leap. It's this limestone ledge that juts out over the water, and it's still there. Some call it Devil's Promenade, but that's the name of the bridge out there too."

I shuddered. I'd read the story online, but coming from this man, told with such conviction, it seemed more real…almost possible.

"Then there's the story about the miner, who was decapitated in a mining accident," Fred interjected. "The light is a lantern he carries, while searching for his head. Then there's the confederate soldier killed by cannon fire, the prospector whose wife was murdered and his children kidnapped by Indians. They say the light is him, searching for his kids."

I jotted notes as they spoke, fascination holding me in its grip. Although I knew, logically, there was a less fantastical explanation for the light, I couldn't help but be swept away in the lore.

I looked up after making my notes. "What about those who say that it's just car lights from the highway?"

Wally shook his head. "My great grandfather seen it when he was a boy of around eight years old, and that was back in 1872, when there weren't no cars on these roads. It was around four in the mornin'. He was heading down to go fishin' in Spring River."

My mouth dropped open. "A child out by himself in the middle of the night?"

"Back then there weren't so much to worry about. Folks let their kids run around." Wally slurped from his coffee cup. "Anyway, he seen it. Couldn't have been headlights back then. And he wasn't no liar."

"Of course." I tried for diplomacy. "I'm sure the people who say they have seen it actually think that they have. I'm not saying they are all liars."

"But you don't believe it exists?"

They all looked at me like I was a dimwitted child.

"No, I'm afraid not. My book is about debunking the supernatural."

Elbur made a harrumph sound. "Missy, I tell you it's as real as I'm sitting here today."

I looked around at the sincere expressions on the elderly men's faces. "So have you all seen it?"

Wally said, "Well, I ain't seen it myself, but I'm the only one out of all of us who hasn't."

I raised my brows. "You haven't seen it? Have you lived in the area your whole life?"

An amused light twinkled in his watery blue eyes. "Well, not yet." He slapped his knee and chortled. His buddies joined him, but I'd guess this wasn't the first time the joke had been used.

I chuckled politely. "If you have lived here all these years, why haven't you seen the light?"

"'Cause," Fred said. "This old goat can't stay up past nine. Never could."

They all laughed again, and I laughed with them. As I finished my donut and coffee, Fred and Elbur told of incidents when they had seen the spook light.

I was impressed by their sincerity. Although I didn't believe for one moment they had seen anything otherworldly, I knew they believed they had.

By the time our meeting ended, I had more information than I anticipated. I was anxious to get back and type it up. I called the inn and asked Loretta to send Holt. While I waited, I called Jillian. I glanced over my shoulder at the kind old men sitting at the table. Elbur noticed me and lifted his hand in a wave. I waved back, and I couldn't help a little niggle of guilt at knowing my book was going to make them look like fools.

****

That night, I decided to check out the spook light myself. Supposedly it could only be seen between the hours of ten p.m. And daylight.

Right at ten p.m., I put on my coat, boots, scarf and gloves then pulled open the front door. I went around back and keyed in the code to the garage door. The door slid open, and I climbed into a golf cart. I headed down the drive, appreciative of the thick plastic that somewhat blocked the wind. Even with the protection, I was chilled by the time I reached the road.

I parked on the shoulder and snuggled into my

coat. Above me, ice-coated tree limbs drooped heavily. A howl rose in the distance. I looked around but saw nothing. Of course, coyotes and mountain lions were sneaky. They wouldn't be parading around in plain view. From what I'd read, they kept mostly away from civilization. Even though this area was hardly what I'd call civilized, it wasn't the wilderness either. I was certain whatever had made that sound was a safe distance away.

A three-quarter moon hung in the sky surrounded by a spattering of stars. Beautiful. I didn't see stars like that in Miami. I focused my attention back to the end of the road. From my understanding, the best spot to see the light was just to the left of a cell tower. I could see the red lights of the tower. I studied the area left of it.

In my peripheral vision, a brief glow appeared. I whipped my head around. A translucent, but not quite human form, wafted above the ditch on the side of the road.

I gasped, and a tremble shot up my legs. *It's not real, whatever I'm seeing, it's not real.*

The figure floated toward me. I lifted the plastic, keeping my gaze on the glow.

What was it?

Not the light. It wasn't in the right spot nor was it the right shape.

I blinked. Still there. Oh God…

I screwed my eyes shut tightly. When I opened them, the glow was gone.

A long sigh escaped me. What had it been? It had to be my imagination. Maybe I'd stared at one spot for too long and it was some kind of refracted light.

Whatever it was, I was done for the night. I'd come

back another time. I'd bring blankets and prepare more thoroughly.

I pulled into the drive of the bed and breakfast. A light in the window drew my attention. A man stood in the frame of the glass looking out. I could tell by his body type, by his bearing, it was Declan Rush. I was too far away to make out his expression, but I sensed a frown of disapproval. Was it because of my late night outing or just me in particular?

No matter. I wasn't here to impress him. I was here to work on my book and prove the spook light was nothing more than a farce.

When I got back inside the house, I headed to the kitchen for a warm drink. Maybe I could scrounge up some hot chocolate. The kitchen light was on, and Jean stood at the stove, stirring a saucepan.

"Howdy, Cami. Everything okay?"

"Yes, fine. I just wanted something warm to drink." I moved beside her. "You're heating milk in a saucepan? Isn't a microwave much quicker and easier?"

She frowned and tsked. "I don't use microwaves. The radiation zaps away all the nutrients."

I kept a straight face and nodded. "I see. Makes sense."

"Want some?"

"Could I maybe have some chocolate in it?" The thought of plain warm milk was not in the least appealing.

"Sure can."

She made a cup of hot chocolate for me and poured her warm milk into a mug. As if by mutual assent, we sat together at the table.

I blew on the hot liquid and took a tentative sip. I

thought about what I'd seen on the road. What the hell had it been? I shuddered and took another drink.

Jean placed a hand over mine where it rested on the table. Her brow furrowed in concern. "Cami, hon. Are you okay?"

I nodded jerkily, but my body still trembled. "I'm fine." I tightened my grip on the handle of the mug. "I was just outside, and I'm still feeling the cold."

"You can tell me the truth." Her voice was gentle, coaxing. "Did something happen out there?"

I swallowed hard. "Do you remember mentioning Eleanor's spirit to me?"

She frowned. "Of course." Her eyes widened. "Why? Did you see her?"

As soon as the words were spoken, I felt even more foolish. I gave a shaky laugh. "It's silly. I mean, I did see something…but it couldn't have been her ghost."

She took a sip from her cup. "Tell me what you saw."

I shook my head. "It was nothing."

"If it was nothing, you wouldn't be shakin' like that."

I bit my lip. "Okay it was some sort of gauzy misty shape. I don't even know how to describe it. At first I thought it was the spook light, but I know now that it wasn't."

Jean blinked rapidly, as if staving off tears. "I've only seen her the one time. And she didn't stay around long enough for me to communicate. If you see her again, will you tell her I'm sorry about what happened and I miss her?"

I stood and shook my head. "You know this is ridiculous. I'm sorry I even said anything. Ghosts do not exist."

Jean stood as well. "Believe what you want to believe. And I know what I believe."

I nodded. Agree to disagree worked for me, as long as we quit discussing it.

We said our good nights, and I headed for the stairs. I turned back to look at Jean. She stood staring at me with a knowing smile that seemed to say, *you might not believe it yet, but eventually, you will.*

Chapter Seven

Late afternoon the next day, I bundled up and headed across the wide yard toward the trees behind the bed and breakfast. The smell of smoke from the fireplace at the inn followed me. The sun was hidden behind the clouds, making the day gloomy, but the wind was calm, and the temperature was slightly warmer than it had been any day since I'd arrived.

I took the path into the woods and surveyed the scenery, which consisted mostly of bare-branched trees and shrubbery. On either side of the trail, snow had accumulated in banks. The trail came to a fork. To the right, through the trees, a shape caught my eye. Some kind of house? But I was sure I was still on Rush property. I took the path to the right toward the structure. As I drew closer, I realized it was a carriage house. How quaint. I had never seen one in person. The white siding had grayed with age and weather. Windows were smudged, and ivy climbed halfway up the sides. Two faded red doors matched the faded red roof.

Wonder what it's used for? They didn't have horses, so they didn't likely have a carriage. The cars were parked in the garage at the house.

I tried one of the doors. Locked. I tried the other. Again, locked. I peeked through windows, but they were covered, or maybe it was just the darkness of the inside. I couldn't make out anything, no shapes or interior of any kind. It might be empty or brimming full for all I could tell.

I was about to turn back when I heard the murmur of a male voice carried on the wind. An irrational prickle of fear swept through me, but I dismissed it. There was nothing to fear out here. Why would there be? Well, maybe coyotes, but what I heard was definitely a human voice.

I stood still and cocked my ear, trying to figure out where the sound came from. It came again. I rounded the carriage house and ended up back where the trail had forked. I took the other path this time.

A glimpse through the trees made me halt. A man stood ten feet away, his back to me. I moved closer and recognized Declan, even though I couldn't see his face. Three headstones were spaced four feet apart. Declan stood in front of a stone looked newer than the others. It was white marble, teardrop-shaped with roses carved into the side.

His sister's grave?

He wore a charcoal gray trench coat with the collar pulled up around his neck. His breath came out like wisps of smoke in the cold air. Snow dampened his dark blonde hair, making it look almost black. He was unaware of my presence. His focus was on the grave.

Sympathy pierced my heart, and I blinked back tears. He looked so forlorn, so alone. I had to tighten my hands into fists inside my coat pockets to keep from reaching out to him. My efforts wouldn't be welcome.

After several moments of silence, I began to wonder if I'd really heard his voice. A small grouping of trees were all that separated this area from the carriage house, so it was possible. But had he been speaking to his sister? He didn't seem the type of man to give in to sentiments such as talking to a dead loved one.

I no sooner had the thought than he spoke again. "I'm sorry, Eleanor. I wish we'd gotten along better, but I did love you. I never wanted this to happen. I only wanted to protect you."

Feeling like a spy and not wanting to continue intruding on his privacy, I stepped back. My foot landed on an icy tree branch lying on the ground, and the sound exploded like a firecracker in the still afternoon.

Declan whirled to look at me.

My heart leapt to my throat.

His expression tightened in anger. "Ms. Burditt? What in God's name are you doing out here?"

"I—I was just…taking a walk." I cast a guilty glance over my shoulder, then looked back at him.

He peered in the direction from which I'd come. "You were at the carriage house?" The words were barked like an accusation.

"Y-yes. I just…" I took a deep breath, suddenly feeling the cold even though the wind was still calm. "I just came upon it. I didn't go in. The doors were locked." I realized my error as soon as I said the words. Too late to take them back.

"You *tried* to get in?" He stalked over until he stood directly in front of me, looming like a dark angry cloud. "The carriage house is off limits. Stay away from it, do you understand me?"

I swallowed. "I wasn't going to hurt anything. I was just curio—"

"I said stay away." His voice was deadly, his eyes molten steel. "Do I make myself clear?"

For one brief moment, the fury in his eyes made me think he *might* be capable of murder after all. Namely, mine. I couldn't speak, so I only nodded. He held my gaze for a few more gut wrenching moments, then stormed away.

Chapter Eight

That evening, I was still licking my wounds after Declan's berating. Was the man rude to everyone, or only me? I should overlook him, I knew—he was grieving, and he apparently felt at least a bit of responsibility for Eleanor's death. He most likely had regrets that made him lash out.

I wondered if my presence was only making things worse for him. Maybe I shouldn't stay the entire two weeks. While being in Florida around my sister and ex-fiancé was torture, being here during a harsh winter with a cold and hostile man wasn't exactly Heaven.

I was heading to my room to work on the book when Loretta intercepted me in the living area. "Camille, I'm glad I found you. You have a phone call."

"Thank you."

I followed Loretta into the library and took the cordless phone, sinking into the soft leather armchair.

"How's the book going?" Jillian said by way of greeting.

"I'm fine," I said sarcastically. "Thank you for asking."

She grunted. "You know I'm going to ask about my baby first. Getting a lot of material? Was my instinct right about the place?"

Jillian had said she had a feeling the place was rife

with people who believed the lore.

"You were right. Although, there are some aspects that are pretty difficult to explain. Things that make the spook light seem legit."

Jillian laughed. "Come on, you aren't going to turn on me and start believing that juju witchcraft nonsense, are you? This book has to really shatter their misconceptions. Make them look like idiots."

"You don't have to phrase it that way. We're just revealing the truth about a silly superstition."

"Yes, and in the meantime, making people who believe that crap look like fools. The more harsh and accurate we are in exploiting their weakness, the better the book sells."

What would she say if I told her what I thought I'd seen? She'd laugh at me. Or worse, take me off the book, thinking I'd lost my skeptic edge. "Yeah, the vibe around here is that the locals believe it. Of course, the Army Corp of Engineers couldn't refute it."

"Doesn't mean it's true."

"Of course not."

There was a pause, then, "I hate to bring up unpleasantness, but I ran into Kathleen at Zumba the other day."

My stomach clenched. I closed my eyes and imagined Kathleen's pretty, smiling face. How I wished I could see it again...be taken back to a time before she'd ripped my heart out. "Oh?"

"She wondered if you were going to make it back in time for the wedding."

I nearly choked. "What did you tell her?"

"I was diplomatic. I didn't tell her you'd rather crawl through hot coals in the nude. I said your assignment was going to take a few weeks, so you wouldn't likely be back."

"I wouldn't care if you did tell her that. Why the hell would she think I'd want to come to hers and Lance's wedding?"

"You know she's always been so wrapped up in herself she's oblivious to others' feelings."

"Yeah, but even a block of stone should have enough sense to know that."

"Ha! You'd think."

I checked my watch. Dinner was in five minutes. "I'd better go. I'll update you on the book soon."

We hung up, and I went into the dining room, surprised to find Declan at the table with Loretta and the Kangs. No new guests had arrived, why was he joining us?

I met his gaze, and he gave me a look that was almost…tender. Maybe he felt bad for the way he'd behaved.

Dinner was delicious, and the conversation enjoyable. My mood lightened. I was happier, or at least more content, than I'd been since my arrival. We all moved to the library after dinner for a nightcap.

Declan approached me as I stood next to the window, sipping brandy. "I wanted to apologize for this afternoon. My behavior was rude and inexcusable."

"Apology accepted. I know you're grieving. And I know you're a private person. I shouldn't have been snooping around."

He shrugged. "I would appreciate it if you'd stay away from the carriage house."

"Of course."

"So, are you finding plenty of material for your

book?"

I sipped the drink to hide my surprise. Suddenly, he was interested in my book? "I've gathered a great deal of information. The locals are quite anxious to talk about the spook light."

He grinned. "Yes, people around here are pretty proud of our less than laudable claim to fame."

"Tell me, honestly, do you believe in the supernatural aspect, or do you think there's a logical explanation?"

He drank from his glass and remained silent for several moments. "I'm not sure what I believe anymore."

I had the feeling he was talking about more than just the spook light. "Have you seen it yourself?"

"When I was in junior high, some of my buddies and I snuck out of the house and got ahold of a bottle of Jim Beam. We came to Spook Light Road, camped out on the shoulder, drank, and watched for the light. My buddies all passed out before I did. I was just about to doze off when something caught my attention. A light. A round ball that sort of hung then bounced for a moment, then drifted away. I woke my friends, but they all said I was just drunk. They didn't believe me. But I knew what I saw. At the time, anyway. As I've gotten older, I convinced myself it didn't happen. Although, and this is the first time I've ever acknowledged it, I'm honestly not sure."

"You think there really could be some mysterious light out there?"

He shrugged. "A lot of people believe it. And, when I saw it back then, I will have to say I did too."

"If nothing else, it makes for interesting

conversation. And, I love the area. It feels so full of…history and life and possibilities."

He smiled. "Your enthusiasm is almost contagious."

We seemed cocooned in our little corner of the library. Jin and Roxanne were deep in conversation with Loretta. Declan gazed down at me, his eyes sparking with an interest I hadn't seen in him before. Or at least it appeared to be interest—the kind a man has for a woman.

I looked away, nervously finished off my brandy, and cleared my throat. "Well, thank you for the apology. I believe I'll turn in for the night."

"Good night, Camille."

My breath stalled in my chest. It was the first time he'd called me by my first name. "Good night."

"If you'd like, I can take you out to the road one evening. We can watch for the light together."

"Really? You'd do that?" Surprise and pleasure filled my heart.

"Sure. Maybe tomorrow night? I'll meet you in the foyer at ten."

"I would love that."

"Good. Tomorrow night it is."

I barely remembered saying good night to the others and heading to my room. My mind whirled. I couldn't stop thinking about the excitement of watching for the spook light with a local. And, as silly as it was, I couldn't help but think of it as a date.

Chapter Nine

The next night, I waited in the foyer for Declan. When he arrived, I couldn't stop a large smile from spreading across my face. It disappeared when I saw the expression on his. Closed, guarded, almost hostile. Back to the same old Declan.

"I'm sorry," he said abruptly. "Something's come up. I won't be able to join you."

I tried to hide my disappointment. "I'll wait if you'll be finished soon." Lord. I sounded pathetic.

"I'm afraid it will be an all-nighter. I've asked Troy to escort you in my place."

I met his gaze. "No need to foist me off on one of your employees. I can go on my own. I don't want to be a bother."

"I'd rather you didn't. It can be dangerous out there alone at night."

I suspected he only said that because he didn't trust me not to attempt to infiltrate the carriage house. "I'm not afraid. I have mace."

He crooked a grin. "Mace will only enrage a coyote."

Warmth stung my cheeks. How did this man always manage to make me feel foolish and fluttery at the same time? "I'll be fine."

"Troy will be here shortly. Let him take you, I insist."

I knew a command when I heard one. Who did he think he was? I didn't want to be rude—even though he seemed to have no qualms about doing so—but I also wouldn't be bossed and bullied. "Oh, but *I* insist it's not necessary. Surely you don't intend to force me to wait on Troy?"

"I won't force you, no. If you're going to be that stubborn, I'll rearrange my plans and go with you." He said it as though he'd agreed to have a root canal without anesthesia.

Rearrange his plans? How would that be possible, when apparently they were so urgent he'd had to cancel ours in order to attend to them? "Never mind. I'm not much in the mood anyway. I'll just stay in."

He narrowed his eyes and studied me as if trying to figure out my degree of sincerity. He nodded. "Very well, then. If you need anything, Loretta or Jean will see to your needs."

"Thank you. Good night, Mr. Rush."

He inclined his head. "Goodnight, Ms. Burditt."

I headed upstairs, and he remained in the foyer. I felt his gaze on my back until I reached the top. No doubt, he was making sure I obeyed his command. I went into my room and shut the door.

I waited fifteen minutes, then eased open the door and hurried down the stairs. I grabbed my coat and slipped out the front door, into the freezing winter night. Who the hell did Declan Rush think he was? I'd be damned if I'd let him dictate where I would go.

Once again, I took a golf cart. I parked on the shoulder and stared toward the end of the road. A distant barking that morphed into a howl brought chills over my flesh. It would serve me right if I were eaten by a coyote as stubborn as I'd acted.

I'd been out for two hours with not even a glimpse of a light...spook light, headlights or otherwise. I yawned, deciding to call it a night, although, if I couldn't hang any longer than this, I would never see the light. Correction, never confirm that I *hadn't* seen the light. Which didn't exist.

I wasn't aware I'd made a conscious decision, but I found myself parking the golf cart at the edge of the woods, at the mouth of the trail that led to the carriage house. What was there that Declan didn't want me to see? I felt a little guilty, but I pushed it away. If he had something valuable, it wasn't like I was going to steal it. And if he was hiding something criminal, the authorities had a right to know.

As before, I tried both doors. As before, neither of them opened. I checked all the windows, this time using the flashlight on my cell to try to penetrate the interior gloom. Nothing. Definitely something covering the windows.

Short of breaking the door down, I was obviously not going to access the carriage house. Why it should matter so much, I didn't know. But with Jean's theories about Eleanor, and Declan's evasiveness, there were too many secrets around here. If one of them was that a murder had taken place and I could find something to point to the killer, it was my duty to report it. Somehow, I *would* get into that carriage house.

I stepped back and turned, then halted with a quick intake of breath. The apparition—and I didn't know what else to call it by now—stood directly in front of me. So close, I could touch it, although I had no desire to do so.

Moving backward, I put out a hand. "Listen, I don't know what's going on here. I assume this is some kind of trick, or maybe I'm losing my mind. But I don't want any trouble—"

My back met the side of the carriage house. Nowhere to go. Trapped. The thing kept coming toward me.

Am I losing my mind?

I saw it, didn't I? When the thing was only inches away, that same extra coldness I'd felt the day of my arrival washed over me. This time, over my whole body. Terror gripped my stomach, and my knees buckled. I pushed my spine against the siding of the house, trying to stay upright. I let out a mewling whimper.

If you cry, it will sense your weakness.

Through quivering lips, I said, "You're not real. Go away, you're not real."

I squeezed my eyes shut. *It's not real. I will count to ten, and when I open my eyes, the terrifying thing will be gone. Please God, let it be gone...*

I counted to ten more quickly than I ever had in my life. Opening my eyes took longer.

A scream burst from my throat, and I clamped my hand over my mouth. It was still there. And I could see clearly enough now that it was a woman...the spirit of a woman. How could this be?

I swallowed and opened my mouth to speak. A rusty croak came out. I tried again. This time, though weak, I had a voice. "Wha—who are you? What do you want?"

The thing just...hovered there. Waiting... for what?

My body trembled so badly my teeth clacked together. I wanted to run, but my legs wouldn't move. It was real. The ghost was real.

I took a deep breath. She couldn't hurt me, right? She was just an amorphous spirit. And, somehow, although she had no discernible features, she looked…sad.

Maybe she was appearing to me for some purpose. "Do you…do you want something…from me?"

The figure moved backward slowly, but still kept its focus on me. As though she wanted me to come with her. I took a tentative step forward. She continued to move slowly. And I continued to follow.

Chapter Ten

The spirit led me to the house after I hurriedly returned the cart to the garage. She floated through the door. I opened it and went inside. I glanced around the foyer. No one was around. What would I do if someone showed up? Would they see the ghost as well? And who was she? Was this Eleanor? Why would she appear to me and not her brother, or Jean, who had been a close friend, but had only caught a glimpse of her once?

The only way I would find answers to my questions was to continue to follow her. I climbed the stairs behind her. She began to move faster, and I picked up my pace to keep up, puffing by the time we reached the first landing. She continued to the next level.

The staff quarters. Where I was told not to go.

The sound of a door opening made me halt. I whirled. Holt was stepping out of a room. My heart crawled into my throat. I turned to check the whereabouts of the ghost, but she had disappeared.

Holt frowned. "Excuse me, what are you doing up here?"

"I—I just..." Just following your dead wife's ghost? I could hardly say that.

He clicked the door shut behind him and came toward me, his fists balled at his sides. His expression was much less friendly than it had been during our last encounter. "Can I help you?"

"N-No, thank you. I'm sorry. I just got turned around. It's a big house, you know."

He nodded. "Well, your room is on the second floor. I'm not sure how you got so turned around you ended up here. You'll need to go back the way you came. I can take you."

I was tired of getting bossed around by men—well, Loretta too. Of course, it was their property, but they acted like I was going to steal something. Or…uncover a secret.

"I know the way. Thank you."

He nodded. "Just a word of warning. Guests aren't allowed up here."

This inn certainly had a lot of rules. "I understand. Sorry."

He grunted an unintelligible reply and eyed me expectantly.

I turned and headed back to the stairs, surreptitiously looking around for the ghost. She was nowhere to be found. Perhaps because she'd already pointed me in the direction she wanted me to go. To Eleanor's husband.

****

The next day at breakfast, Jean and I were once more the only ones in the kitchen. I dug into the delicious eggs and ham she'd prepared.

Trying to sound casual, although after searching my mind, I couldn't think of a casual way to broach the topic, I said, "So, did Eleanor and Holt have a good marriage?"

Jean paused and leveled a look on me. "Why do

you ask?"

I shrugged. "I just…wondered. He must be devastated at losing her. But, I don't know. He seems more…angry than sad."

"Has he been rude to you? We've had complaints from guests before about his attitude. I'll speak to Mr. Rush."

"No, that's not necessary. He wasn't rude. I've just noticed his demeanor is sometimes a little…defensive."

"I think I might know a little about that." Jean dried her hands on a towel and came over and sat beside me. "I don't like to speak out of turn, but I like you. You're friendly, not like a lot of the guests who come through here and treat me like I'm nothing but a servant."

I smiled. "I like you too. I don't want you to tell me anything that makes you uncomfortable."

She poured a cup of coffee for herself and blew on it before taking a drink. "Eleanor and Holt married right out of high school. They'd dated all through junior high. They seemed happy at first. But Holt wanted a baby. Eleanor didn't. Her dream was to turn the Rush family home into a bed and breakfast, and she became obsessed with the plan. Mr. Rush was against it, but he let her talk him into it, as long as she took care of the running, and he didn't have to deal with the guests. Holt was pushed to the back burner. He began to resent it. Started having affairs."

I frowned. "Did Eleanor know about the affairs?"

Jean nodded. "Sure she did. You can't keep secrets in a town this small."

I wasn't so sure about that. Someone was keeping secrets. I knew it. There was more to Eleanor's death than the authorities thought. "Why didn't they just get a divorce?"

Jean sighed. "I guess because they'd always been together. It had become more a habit than anything else. If Eleanor had lived, they might have wound up divorced. Who knows?"

"Were they fighting before she died?"

Jean slurped from her coffee cup and squinted at me. "You think her death wasn't an accident."

How could I tell her that when I didn't know myself? What could I say, it was just a feeling? One I'd had ever since I met Eleanor's ghost. "I didn't say that. I'm just being nosy. You know, a writer's curse. Our imagination never stops."

"Except you write non-fiction. You deal in facts."

Touché. "To be honest, I do have this…feeling." I couldn't tell her about the ghost. Even though she'd mentioned the possibility herself. I certainly wasn't ready to say it out loud. "Some kind of sense that there's more to her death than we know."

Tears came to Jean's eyes. She wiped them with the hem of her apron. "Poor dear. I hate the thought that someone killed her. I especially hate the thought Holt had anything to do with it. I've known that boy all his life. I trusted him."

I heard a *but* in her voice. I placed a hand over hers. "You know something. Tell me."

She wrapped her hands around her cup and stared into the dark liquid. "A few nights before her death, I woke up in the wee hours. I don't know why, but I had this unsettled kinda feeling. I got out of bed and came downstairs to make a warm cup of milk."

She fell silent, and I waited. A sound at the door

caught my attention. I turned and saw a flash of movement. "Did you hear something?" I asked Jean.

"No, did you?"

"I thought I did." I rose and went to the door. I looked out into the hallway. No one was around. "I guess not." I returned to my chair. "Sorry. Go on."

"I was heating my milk, and I heard voices. Mad voices. A man and a woman. Arguing." She rubbed a hand over her mouth. "It was him and Eleanor. They was saying awful things to each other. And…" She took a deep breath. "And, he threatened her."

"Oh my God. Threatened to kill her?"

"He told her if she told anyone, she'd be sorry."

"Told anyone what?"

"I don't know. I didn't hear everything. I just heard rage in his voice."

I tightened my hands to keep them from shaking. Her husband threatened her in a rage. And a few nights later, she was dead. "Did you tell the police?"

Jean shook her head. "I couldn't bring myself to say anything. I still didn't believe in my heart he'd hurt her, and I couldn't cause any more pain for the family. They'd suffered enough."

"Perhaps." My voice rang hollow. "But no one suffered as much as Eleanor."

Chapter Eleven

Two nights before Valentine's Day, it suddenly hit me. I hadn't thought about Lance and Kathleen in days, but the time had arrived—day after tomorrow, my sister would be marrying my ex-fiancé. The only man I'd ever loved. And he would now be my brother-in-law. Like an idiot, I'd packed my engagement ring. I dug it out of the side pocket of my luggage and clutched it in my fingers. Tears squeezed from my eyes, and I angrily wiped them away.

Throwing a green silk robe over another of my ratty nightshirts—this one an Elvis shirt I'd gotten a few years ago on a trip to Graceland—I headed downstairs to the library. Maybe I'd read. Or find some booze.

When I opened the library door, the scent of vanilla reached me and I noticed the faint flicker of a candle. I looked across the dimly lit room to find Declan, his back to me, standing at the window, staring outside at the snow slapping against the panes.

I hesitated, knowing I should leave, but I really wanted a drink. I stood for a while debating. I wasn't sure if I'd made a sound, but he turned and saw me.

His eyes narrowed. "What are you doing?"

"Wha—I… I couldn't sleep."

He crossed the room and stopped in front of me. He was sans jacket, and his white dress shirt was

171

partially unbuttoned, his dark blonde hair mussed. "So you thought you'd just roam the house, wily nily?"

I scowled. "You know, I've never experienced such rudeness from people who run a business that caters to guests. Everywhere I go, someone tells me it's off limits." I lifted my chin and stared into his angry face. "From my understanding, the library is accessible to guests."

"Perhaps. But I'm in a foul mood." He shook his nearly empty glass at me. Ice clinked loudly. "And I've been drinking." A nasty smile curved his full lips. "And when I drink, I'm not the gentle teddy bear I normally am."

I smirked and forced myself to be calm, even though my heart fluttered in my chest. "Well, I'm not afraid of you. And I'm not exactly in a hospitable mood myself." Without forethought, I took the drink from his hand and downed the contents in one gulp. The liquor—scotch, I thought, but I wasn't familiar with the taste—burned my throat, but I kept it from showing on my expression.

He stared at me in shock for several moments, then grinned. "It looks like we're going to need more booze."

He moved to the liquor cabinet and took out a bottle of scotch and another glass. He poured the amber liquid into each glass. Moving back to me, he handed me one of the drinks. He raised his toward me, and I clinked my glass against it. We drank, eyeing each other.

"So, what are we drinking to?" I asked.

"How about to regrets and ruminations."

"I'll drink to that." I choked back another slug of

the scotch. This time, it went down easier.

He stepped closer and gazed at me intently, a frown creasing his brows. Reaching out, he placed his hand against my cheek. I gasped in surprise. He lifted my face and stared into my eyes. "Have you been crying?"

I blinked and pulled back. "No, I haven't been crying. The scotch just made my eyes burn."

I moved away and settled onto the soft, plush sofa. He followed me and lowered down next to me. Although nearly a foot separated us, I still felt the warmth of his body. I resisted the urge to shift away from him. He'd see it as weakness.

"Look, if you don't want to tell me, that's fine. But we're both having trouble sleeping. We're drinking. Drinking loosens the tongue. You'll tell me eventually." He refilled my glass. "I'll keep plying you with booze until you do."

I laughed. What would be wrong with telling him? He was right. Already, the booze had relaxed me. And I wanted to talk to someone about it. Why not Declan Rush, who would never engage in gossip?

I took another drink of the scotch and swallowed. "I was engaged to be married. Lance and I had been going out for five years, and he'd finally popped the question. Our wedding was set for Valentine's Day."

"*This* Valentine's Day?"

I gave a grim smile. "Yes, this Valentine's Day. It's that recent."

"I assume, since you're here, and tomorrow is Valentine's Day, the wedding isn't going to happen?"

"No, it's going to happen."

He raised his brows. "But you're here."

"Right. Lance is marrying my sister."

Shock flashed over his face. "Your sister? Damn. That smarts."

I chuckled. "Yeah, it smarts all right." I brought my glass to my lips, surprised to discover it was empty. I frowned.

Silently, he refilled it. "I'm sorry. You must be devastated."

I drew in a trembling breath. "I am. But you know, my sister's betrayal hurts so much worse than his. I mean, we were never close, but I love her. I thought she loved me." I noticed my words had started to slur. Maybe I'd had enough to drink. But I took another gulp.

"I'm sure she loves you."

I looked at him. "Oh? Then why did she steal my fiancé?"

He pursed his lips in concentration. "Maybe she's just a selfish bitch?"

I burst out laughing, suddenly feeling better. I didn't know if it was the booze or talking to Declan. But somehow, the hurt had eased. "So. How about you tell me something about you. How come you're so surly?"

The humor left his face. I could feel him closing off. I must have hit a nerve.

"Sorry." I stood. "I don't mean to pry. I'll leave you alone."

He took my hand and lowered me down next to him. "No. It's okay. I'll tell you."

I tried not to focus on the warm electricity that skittered over my flesh at his touch. Instead, I concentrated on the fact that he was going to open up to me. I waited breathlessly.

"My sister and I grew up in this town. We've lived here our entire lives. We had friends, a good place in the community. Respect. But that all ended ten years ago."

"What happened?"

"My father killed a woman."

I couldn't help the gasp that left my throat. "He—murdered someone? Who?"

Declan frowned into his glass and took another sip. "Her name was Victoria Carr. I don't know exactly what happened. Apparently, they had some kind of history. We never knew why. But he was convicted."

"He's in prison?"

Declan shook his head. "He's dead. He shot himself in the head the day his trial ended."

Oh my God. His father. His sister. Had Eleanor killed herself too? Was there something in the family genes? No, of course not. His father had a reason—if anyone ever had a reason to commit suicide. He didn't want to face life in prison. What reason would Eleanor have had? She'd finally seen her dream of opening the bed and breakfast come true.

"I'm so sorry."

He nodded. "Afterward, the town turned on Eleanor and me. You'd think *we* had murdered Victoria Carr."

"Why did you stay?"

"I didn't want to. But Eleanor was determined to reclaim our place in the community. She convinced me to turn our family home into this inn. I couldn't refuse her. It meant the world to her."

"You and your sister were close?"

He grimaced a smile. "I loved my sister very much. And, we were close, but I'm afraid we didn't get along all that well."

"Why?"

He gave a slow shrug. "I don't know. She had a lot of resentment toward me. My father's will left a majority of the inheritance to me. I assured her I would share it evenly once I got it. I don't inherit the entire fortune until I turn thirty this June. But it ate at her that Dad didn't split it evenly. And I don't know if she believed I'd make good on my promise. She died before I inherited it."

I drained my glass, and when Declan didn't make a move to refill it, I did it myself. My head had started to spin. But I wasn't feeling as inebriated as I had moments ago. The horror of Declan's story had sobered me.

"I'm sorry."

He grinned. "You already said that."

"I guess I don't know what to say. You've been through so much." I didn't realize I was crying until he reached up and thumbed tears off my cheeks.

"You're sweet." His hand remained on my face. His gaze dropped to my mouth, and I stopped breathing.

He was silent for several moments. Was he going to kiss me? Even in my inebriated state, I knew that it would be a mistake. We'd both had too much to drink. And we didn't even *like* each other.

I rose quickly to my feet. I swayed and brought a hand to my temples. "Oh my." Dizziness swam, and I closed my eyes, but that only made it worse.

Declan stood. "Are you okay?"

"I'm fine." I took a step. "I just need to lie down." I took another step, and my knees buckled.

"Here, I'd better get you to bed." Before I knew his intention, Declan swept me up in his arms and carried me out of the library and up the stairs. I should have protested, but it was so warm against his chest. I had to resist the urge to wrap my arms around his neck and snuggle into him.

He stopped in front of my door, and I turned the knob and pushed it open. We stepped inside. The room closed around us, giving an intimate feel that was thick with sexual tension. Foolishly, I didn't want him to release me.

He didn't until he reached my bed, where he lowered me gently onto the spread.

"Are you okay?" His voice rumbled like the low hum of a motor in the stillness of the room.

I sat up and took his face in my hands. The gray in his eyes burned with a metallic force. I felt as though if I came any closer, I'd incinerate. And the thought was delicious.

"Declan," I whispered.

He drew in a sharp breath. I wasn't sure who moved first, but the next thing I knew, he was sitting next to me on the bed, and our lips were touching. His arms went around me, and he deepened the kiss. A shiver shot through my body, warming me to my core. My skin tingled, and I felt as though I'd burst if I didn't get closer…didn't get more…

Declan gripped my hands and pulled them from his face. He abruptly stood and stared down at me, his breath ragged, his gaze sizzling through me.

"I think I'd better go." The words sounded

squeezed out of him.

"Why?"

He closed his eyes and shook his head. "Because, you've had too much to drink." He opened his eyes. "And perhaps I haven't had enough."

His words brought a sting of tears to my eyes. I was sober enough to know he meant he'd have to be inebriated to want me. Fine, that was just freaking fine...

"Please close the door when you leave." I tried to keep tears from my voice but I didn't succeed.

"Camille, I'm sorry. I—"

"Just go. You're right. I've had too much to drink. And now, I just need to sleep." Still wearing my robe, I slid beneath the covers as if to prove my point.

He remained by the bed for a few moments. I screwed my eyes tightly shut, not drawing a full breath until I heard the door close behind him.

Chapter Twelve

I didn't see Declan the next day, and I told myself I was relieved, but that contradicted the pang in my heart.

I lay down for a nap that afternoon, determined to give the spook light watch another try, and wanting to be well rested when I did.

Packing a blanket, a sandwich, cookies, a Coleman lamp, and coffee, I took the golf cart out to the road and parked on the shoulder, next to a wire fence. Nervous anticipation filled me at the thought I might actually see the spook light tonight. And, I now believed it, completely. How could I write a book debunking something that I knew to be true? Jillian would be furious. On the other hand, maybe she would be satisfied with a book written from another perspective, a book about *true* paranormal sightings? Not likely. Jillian didn't have a reputation for being flexible.

I did know that I could no longer write the book I had planned to write. If ghosts were real then I couldn't deny this spook light could possibly be real. I would stay out here all night if I had to. I wasn't sure how I would keep from freezing to death in the process, but I was going to give it a shot.

The blackness around me was broken only by the blinking of the cell tower lights ahead and the glow of moonlight. In spite of my coat and the blanket I'd wrapped around my shoulders, frigid air seeped through my skin all the way to my bones. From a distance came the low rumble of cars and a keening sound I was growing accustomed to. The possibility of coyotes no longer frightened me—at least not as much as it had in the beginning—but the haunted wail still sent a shiver through my body.

I'd been out for hours when my lids grew heavy, in spite of the nap I'd taken. I poured the last of the coffee from the thermos into the cup and drank the lukewarm liquid. I checked my phone, which was only good as a clock now that I had no service. Four a.m. Six hours. If I hadn't seen it by now, I probably wouldn't see it at all.

I stared down the road, stretching my eyes wide to keep them open. I wasn't going to make it. I was so sleepy…

I yawned so hard my jaw ached. Definitely time to go in. I reached for the golf cart key, then stopped mid-motion when a glimmer of light caught my eye. I jerked my head up.

There…at the end of the road between the overhang of skeletal tree branches, an orange-yellow ball of light appeared. It hung in the air for a moment before moving in a bouncy motion from left to right.

Oh wow… Was I really seeing it?

I blinked and looked again.

The light was still there.

I jumped out of the cart. "Oh my God. The spook light," I whispered in awe.

I no longer felt the cold, and I was no longer sleepy. My insides jittered, but from excitement rather than fear. In one of the articles I'd read, a psychic claimed the light wasn't actually a light, but a dimension to another world…that it could lead to danger. But still, I wasn't afraid.

This was amazing. Beyond amazing. I fumbled out my cell phone and snapped a few photos. I touched the thumbnail and breathed a sigh of relief. Unlike Eleanor had in the video, the light hadn't disappeared. I'd actually gotten pictures.

I glanced around, feeling alone, wishing someone were here to share it with me. I let out a scoffing chuckle. *Be honest, you wish Declan were here to share it with you.*

In spite of my humiliation, I hadn't been able to stop thinking about him since last night. I couldn't help but wonder how he would treat me when we saw one another again. No doubt, after my clumsy attempt to hit on him, it would be awkward to say the least.

I hung out for another half an hour, until the spook light disappeared. I was disappointed, but I'd known it wouldn't last forever. At least I had seen it. And I had pictures.

Jillian *had* to let me write this new book. Now, I could prove that the spook light existed. And, knowing it was real, I could make the book an even more entertaining read by sharing the legends.

I climbed into the cart and headed back to the inn, my mind brimming with possibilities now that I had an entirely new outlook on the phenomenon. I couldn't wait to revise the book.

****

Valentine's Day arrived, and I had yet to see Declan. Perhaps he planned to stay out of sight until I left. The thought embarrassed and saddened me.

Jean was making a special, private Valentine's Day dinner for Jin and Roxanne. I was informed I could still eat in the dining room, but that certainly did not sound appealing.

I'd told Loretta I'd just skip dinner.

I showered, slipped on my green silk robe and headed back toward my room. A figure loomed at the end of the hallway, and I yelped.

"Camille? Everything okay?"

Declan, thank God. My heartbeat slowed, and I let out a sound that was part laugh, part relieved sigh. "I'm fine. You just scared me."

"I'm sorry, I didn't mean to."

"What are you doing on this floor?"

"Looking for you. I wondered if you wanted to join me for dinner."

I barked out a laugh. "You want to have dinner with me? I mean, we're not exactly best friends, and we're definitely not a romantic couple. Do you realize it's Valentine's Day?"

"Exactly. I thought we could have a non-valentine's dinner."

I frowned in confusion. "A non-valentine's dinner?" In spite of myself, I was intrigued. "What did you have in mind?"

"Thumbing our noses at the sappy tradition. If you're in, throw on something sloppy and comfortable, and meet me in the dining room."

I grinned. A wave of near giddy happiness swept over me. Not only was Declan not avoiding me, we were having dinner together, even if it was a dinner with the full intention of being *non*-romantic. It would still be with him. "I have just the thing."

In my room, I pulled on sweats and a Florida Marlins jersey and headed down to the dining room.

I stepped inside and burst out laughing.

Black crepe paper was looped around the room. Beheaded cupids hung on the walls. The Rolling Stones' "Sympathy for the Devil" played.

Declan wore a faded, gray, Red Sox T-shirt and jeans with holes in them and still managed to look incredibly sexy.

"This is awesome," I said. I pointed to our attire. "And we are both wearing MLB shirts, how about that?"

He chuckled. "I noticed. You look appropriately…sloppy."

"Thank you, so do you."

His gaze flickered over me, and he quirked a grin. "But damn if you don't pull off sloppy."

My mouth went dry, and I grabbed a plastic cup of water off the table and quickly drank.

The table was set with mismatched dinnerware. Two empty jelly glasses sat next to a bottle of vodka, as did a bottle of club soda and a plate of sliced limes.

He indicated the chair next to me. "Sit, I'm not going to pull it out for you."

I gave him a grin and plopped in the chair. "I'd punch you if you did."

He pointed to the vodka. "I figured we still needed booze, just not wine or champagne. You know, too romantic."

"Good call." I squinted at the two silver domes covering plates. "But what's this? Looks like a romantic dinner to me."

"You think so?" He lifted the cover off my plate.

In a French accent that would rival that of a chef at a five-star restaurant, he said, "Here, we 'ave zee delectable hot dogs, smothered in chopped onionz." He swept a hand over the plate. "Accompanying zis fine entrée, you will zee garlic infused French fries."

I laughed. "Nothing says romance like onions and garlic."

He winked and flutters went through my belly. "That's what I'm thinking."

"This is great. The best non-valentine's day ever."

"I think we just invented a new holiday."

He knew how difficult today was for me. I was touched. "Thank you for being so nice."

He gave a humorless smile. "If I hadn't been such an ass all this time, you wouldn't have to thank me for being nice."

I smiled. "Good point."

Dinner was oddly relaxed. We ate and talked and laughed, and while I wasn't a fan of hot dogs, they were somehow delicious.

After dinner, he handed me a sealed envelope.

"What's this?"

"Non-valentine's day wouldn't be complete without a card."

I gave him a skeptical look but opened the envelope and slid the card out. On the front were the words "Unhappy Non-Valentine's Day." Where would he have gotten such a card? He must have made it on the computer himself. Inside was an image of a zombie feasting on a cupid and it read, "Love bites."

I laughed. "I love it. It's perfect."

He laughed too, then sobered. "I really am sorry about tonight. I know you must be thinking about the wedding."

Strangely, I hadn't thought about Lance or

Kathleen once since I'd walked into the room, but I didn't want Declan to know that. "Yes, you're right. This evening has helped take my mind off it."

"Good." He grinned. "I would ask you to dance, but that's too romantic, don't you think?"

"Oh yes, absolutely." Although, the thought of being held in his arms was tempting to say the least. "So, what do you suggest?"

"Come on, let's go outside."

I was reluctant to leave the warm, cozy atmosphere, but I would have followed him to Hades.

We bundled up and trudged outside, where we made ice snowballs and threw them at tree branches, knocking icicles off. The splatter and bursting of the ice as we shattered it was oddly satisfying.

My face was numb, and my feet were as frozen as the icicles we'd destroyed by the time we quit. But I went to bed that night, warmer and happier than I had been in a long time. Declan had shown a side of himself that I never would have believed existed.

He'd done it to help me forget. But I couldn't help but wonder if he was trying to forget about something himself.

****

I woke the next morning, rested and refreshed. I'd gotten the first full night's sleep since my arrival. I wasn't sure how much it had to do with the vodka I'd consumed the night before, and how much it had to do with the amazing evening I'd had with Declan.

It occurred to me that I hadn't seen Eleanor in a few days. Not since she'd led me to Holt. Was she gone for good, or was I supposed to investigate him on my own?

Maybe I should go into town and do a little digging. I could get Holt to drive me to the library, and while I was at it, perhaps learn a little bit more about his wife.

I found Loretta in her office and knocked on the open door.

She looked up at me with a tight smile. "Hello, Camille. How are you?"

"I'm fine, you?"

"Good. Thank you." She tapped a pen on top of the desk. "Did you and Declan have a nice evening last night?"

I shifted self-consciously. I was certain she had a thing for Declan. Well, she had no need to worry. I didn't have designs on him. He was sexy, true. And, now that I was getting to know another side of him, I found him even more attractive. But, I was only here for five more days. Besides, I was not looking for a relationship, and I knew he wasn't either.

"Yes. It was nice, thank you."

"I found his choice of menu rather strange."

"He wanted to have a—" I clamped my mouth shut. I did not want to explain to Loretta. The evening belonged only to me and Declan. "A casual dinner," I finished.

Loretta inclined her head. "Well, hot dogs and French fries are certainly casual."

"Yes, they are." Before she could grill me further, I said, "Listen, I would like to go to town this afternoon. Is Holt available to drive me?"

"Of course. He'd be happy to. What time?"

"As soon as he's available."

"One moment." She picked up the phone, and I

186

waited while she made the call. She hung up and smiled. "He'll be down in half an hour."

"Thank you."

True to his word, Holt arrived in the lobby thirty minutes later. He wore a flannel shirt with a Carhart coat and a ball cap that proclaimed, "I'd rather be fishing" pulled over his reddish-brown hair.

"We have a library at the inn," he said after we were settled in the car. "But you want to go to the one in town?"

"Yes I need to have computer access and do some research. For my book," I hastily added and then wondered if I'd sounded like I was guilty of something.

We'd driven for a few miles when I said, "I am so sorry. I heard what happened to your wife."

His jaw tightened, and his knuckles turned white on the steering wheel. "Thank you."

"You must miss her terribly."

He shot a glare at me. I could tell he wanted to be rude, but he said calmly, "Yes, of course. She was my wife."

I felt bad that I had to keep pushing. "It's crazy. Such a bizarre accident. Her drowning even though she was a strong swimmer…"

He slowly nodded. "Yes. Bizarre."

"I hate to bring up anything unpleasant, but have you ever wondered if maybe…" I let the words die. I had gone too far. Who was this pushy, intrusive person I'd become?

He expelled a loud breath. "Wondered what? If she was murdered?"

I flinched. "I'm sorry. I shouldn't have brought it up."

"It's okay. I've wondered about that myself."

His statement took me by surprise. If he had killed her, surely he wouldn't be so quick to admit she might have been murdered. Unless he was putting the blame on someone else?

"But the authorities ruled it an accident," I said. "I guess they didn't have any evidence to say otherwise?"

"Maybe they should have dug a little deeper."

"Did you tell them that?"

He let out a derisive grunt. "I did, but they just blew me off as the grieving husband."

"Do you have some kind of evidence that would show her death was not an accident?"

He was silent for a moment as he scowled out the windshield where the wipers were struggling to keep snow and ice away. Outside was nothing but a blur of white. Only a few other cars were on the road. It felt so...isolated. What was wrong with me? I was alone with a potential killer, and I was goading him to discuss the victim? Maybe I should have thought this through more carefully.

"Nothing I can prove," he finally said.

I swallowed nervously but decided to press my luck. "Did you and Eleanor get along well?"

He gave a melancholy smile. "Ha, I loved Eleanor, but she didn't get along *well* with anyone. At least not for very long."

"So you two fought a lot?"

"Oh, yeah. We had some doozies. We'd have fought a lot more, except I usually just did what she wanted and kept my mouth shut."

If he had killed her, why was he opening up about their tempestuous relationship? "Still, you must have loved her very much to have stayed with her."

"I did. I've loved her since the first time I laid eyes on her in fifth grade."

Silence fell between us. I wasn't sure what else to say. I was hoping to learn something that would clue me in as to what really happened to his wife. Not that I thought he was going to confess, and I wasn't sure I wanted him to. If he did, he would probably kill me. But I hoped he'd drop some kind of hint I could follow up on.

When he spoke again, I was so deep in thought, I jumped.

"You know I wasn't the only one who fought with Eleanor."

"Who else did she fight with?"

"Her brother. Well, really, the two of them didn't actually *fight* much. Declan wouldn't usually engage with her, which pissed her off, let me tell you." He chuckled. "But they didn't get along. Sometimes, I almost felt that Eleanor hated him."

Chills rushed over my skin. "Hate? That is a pretty strong emotion for a sister to feel about her brother."

"She resented the hell out of him for keeping from her what was rightfully hers. She worked her fingers to the bone on the bed and breakfast, and all she would ever own was a part of it. He had no interest in it at all, yet he kept control of the whole thing. It was like he rubbed her face in the fact that she was dependent on what he gave her."

I was surprised to find myself coming to his defense. "It was my understanding that he was against even turning it into a bed and breakfast, but he did it because his sister wanted it."

He glowered at me. "Of course you're going to defend him. I see how cozy you two are getting. And I haven't seen Declan get cozy with no one in a long time. Not since that business with his father."

"We're not getting cozy at all."

He ignored my protest. "And as far as him turning this into a bed and breakfast, what she really wanted was to be an artist. He stifled her dreams and kept her from leaving this place."

This was different than what I'd heard—that he'd stayed *for* her. I was sure that somewhere between both versions of the story was the truth.

When Holt dropped me off at the library, I logged onto the computer. I was like a child discovering a box of candy-coated toys. It seemed forever since I'd actually been connected to the Internet. I checked my email and Facebook, but only quickly skimmed them. I was anxious to research Eleanor's death and the incident with Declan's father. I put in the words Rush, Quapaw, murder and the year 2006, since Declan had said it was ten years ago. I found several articles and clicked on one.

Benjamin Rush was convicted of murdering Victoria Carr. She was from the area but had moved away. No one knew of her return until she was found dead. She had a son who still lived in Detroit.

No motive was ever determined. Benjamin Rush was out on bond but didn't show up to court when the verdict was read. He'd shot himself, in his home, that day.

Sadness filled my soul. Such a tragedy for everyone concerned. The woman, her son, Declan, Eleanor, and even their father.

I googled Eleanor's name. I read the article about the day she'd been found. Holt himself had found her. How awful. No new information came up about her death. I logged off the computer and sat back in my chair.

Had Declan really forced her to stay? If he'd stifled her dreams then that would definitely cause hostility between them.

But was it enough hostility to drive him to murder?

Chapter Thirteen

Eleanor came to me again that night. I was just about to doze off when the sensation of her presence permeated the room. Her spirit was at the foot of my bed, and I sat up, my heart beating out of control. Although I believed she wouldn't harm me, I couldn't stop the trickle of fear that skated over my skin.

"Eleanor?" I said, my voice shaky. "What is it?"

She simply hovered there, not moving. As if once again waiting. I knew she wanted me to go with her. I climbed from bed and dressed in warm clothes. Downstairs, I bundled up in my coat, then followed Eleanor out the door.

The day had been slightly warmer, but the night was frigid, the ground sheeted with ice. I wasn't sure how far we were going, but I went to the garage to get a cart, just in case. Eleanor couldn't feel the cold, but I could.

I'd just started down spook light road when, over the sound of the wind and the rattling of plastic, I thought I heard something else...like the crunch of footsteps. Fear seized my chest. Was someone out here with me? Following me? I didn't see a thing. Maybe I was imagining it. I gave a wry smile. Funny that I was frightened by an unidentified noise that I *might* have heard when I was literally following a ghost down a road that was darker than the depths of hell.

Eleanor led me down spook light road for a mile or so, then right onto Route 630. The cold wind whipped the plastic hanging on either side of me, sounding like the wings of a gigantic prehistoric bird. I tried to burrow deeper in my coat as icy air froze my flesh. Where was she taking me? Nervousness settled in my stomach. As far as I knew, she could be leading me to my death.

But I must not have truly believed it, because I continued to follow.

We'd gone just over half a mile, and I didn't realize until I saw the moonlight glint off the surface of the water, that we'd arrived at Spring River.

Was she taking me to the place where she'd drowned? I shuddered and swallowed hard. I must be losing my mind to blindly follow her out here.

I parked and climbed from the cart, surprised when, instead of turning toward the water, she headed to a line of trees farther up the bank. I followed her into the woods. She halted next to a large boulder. I walked over to her and realized I was closer to her now than I'd been since the day she first appeared to me. I could feel that extra odd coolness emanating from her, and I shivered.

I glanced around. "I'm not sure what you're wanting me to find here, what you're trying to show me." It was dark in the trees, and I wished I had brought a flashlight. Then, I remembered the flashlight app on my cell phone, which was in my coat pocket.

I fished out my cell and clicked on the flashlight. It was almost eerier with that shaft of light shining among the frozen, darkened landscape.

I shone the light on Eleanor, hoping I could see

something more of her, but she faded back out of the light. "Okay, sorry. I guess you don't like light."

I swept the beam on the ground, walking around the rock and searching as thoroughly as I could. When I'd completely circled the rock twice, I let out a frustrated sigh. "I'm sorry, Eleanor. I don't see what you're trying to show me. I can't imagine there's anything out here to find. Law enforcement would have covered the area thoroughly."

Although, they would have been looking at the spot where she'd drowned. Would they have come this far back?

I walked around for a few more moments, but nothing caught my attention. I was about to give up and turn my flashlight off when a glint of something at the base of the rock snagged my eye. I squatted down and shoved my fingers into the snow. I pulled out a silver chain. With a key charm dangling from it.

I drew in a sharp breath. This was what she wanted me to find. It was the necklace she had been wearing in the photo. And it was broken. Perhaps during a struggle? I looked around for more items but found nothing. I frowned. This was a good distance from where she'd died. Was this the proof I needed? If she hadn't met with foul play, how did her necklace end up here, so far from where she'd died?

I shoved the pendant in my pocket and stood. "Okay, I get it. You're definitely trying to tell me something."

Hurrying to the golf cart, I climbed in and headed back to the house. Eleanor was no longer with me. I'd have to find my way back on my own. My heart ached at what she'd suffered. I hadn't known her, and maybe she wasn't a kind person, but no one deserved what had happened to her. And, exactly what *had* happened to her? All I knew was that she had died. And that it wasn't an accident.

I was hurrying up on the porch when arms grabbed me from behind. I yelped and whirled around, my fingers scrambling in my coat pocket for the mace.

My fright eased when I recognized Troy.

"Camille, are you okay?"

I took a deep breath and let it out slowly. "Yes, sure, I'm fine. Why?"

"You were running like your life depended on it." He peered behind me into the snowy darkness. "Is something chasing you?"

Something... A shudder rippled over my spine. Was whatever had gotten to Eleanor a something, rather than a someone? A coyote, mountain lion? Or was it human? Or, considering he or she was a murderer, *inhuman.*

"No, nothing." I gave a shaky laugh. "I'm just cold. I wanted to get inside where it's warm."

"Of course, sorry." He released me and stepped back.

I turned to go into the house, but a thought made me pause. "Troy?" I looked back at him, my brows raised. "Where were you coming from?"

"What do you mean?"

"You're out here, alone, at night? Did you go for a walk or something?" I thought about asking him about the necklace, about how well he knew Eleanor, but that would sound accusatory.

His eyes narrowed. "I walked around, checking the grounds. I do that every night. It's part of my job."

"Oh, that's right. So, you stayed on the property, you weren't out on the road?"

He crossed his arms. "What's this all about? Are you accusing me of something?"

"No...no, of course not." What was I thinking? If he were a killer, baiting him was not a good idea. "I just heard something when I was walking down the road. I wasn't sure if it was an animal, or a person." I forced a casual laugh. "I was certainly hoping it was you, as I'm sure you understand."

His stance relaxed, and he smiled. "Yes, I understand. But I'm afraid it wasn't me." He gestured with his arm out toward the wilderness. "You need to be careful roaming around on your own out here. Not much crime in this area, but that doesn't mean there isn't any danger."

"Right. Thanks for the warning." What an understatement. Ghosts, coyotes, suspicious deaths. Danger was all around. The question was, from what, or whom, should I fear it the most?

****

The next morning at breakfast, I was alone in the kitchen with Jean. I couldn't keep this to myself. I had to tell someone. And she was the only one I trusted.

"Jean...can I ask you something?"

"Sure you can." She settled next to me at the table. "What is it?"

I'd brought the necklace with me, and I felt its presence in my jeans pocket. "I saw a photo of Eleanor wearing a beautiful pendant. Do you know, was it special to her?"

She smiled wistfully. "I'll say. It was a family heirloom, passed down for generations. And worth a small fortune, I might add. Her mother gave it to her just before she died."

"Wow, that is special."

"Yeah. Them black stones are Spinels. Have you heard of 'em?" When I shook my head, she continued, "They're kinda rare, at least certain ones are. They come in every color you can imagine. Black Spinels are for protection, to get rid of negativity and resentment. Eleanor loved the necklace, but I don't think it cured her of all that. Anyway, she never took it off."

"Was she...wearing it when they found her body?"

Her expression turned sad. "As far as I know, it was never recovered. I suppose it was lost in the water."

I considered for a moment. "But what if it wasn't?"

Jean's brows rose. "What do you mean?"

"Can I trust you? Really trust you?"

She pursed her lips. "That's something you'll have to decide. Of course I'm gonna tell you that you can trust me. You have to decide if you believe me."

I smiled. "Wise woman." With a deep breath, I reached into my pocket and pulled out the necklace. I showed it to her.

Her eyes widened, and she sprang to her feet. "What the...?" She put a hand to her heart. "Is that...that's Eleanor's."

I nodded. "I know."

"Where did you get it?"

I told her everything. About all the visits from Eleanor and about her leading me to the necklace.

"Dear God." She sank back down into the chair. "My poor little Eleanor. She must have been terrified." She shook her head. "I can't imagine some monster..."

"Should we tell the police?"

Jean was silent for a moment, then shook her head. "No. Not yet. We need more to go on. We'll just hold onto the necklace until we have something else."

"But…it seems wrong to keep it from them. Shouldn't we at least tell Declan?"

"No!" The word came out sharp, and she softened her voice. "He's been through enough. Let's make sure we have everything we need before we upset anyone."

"Okay, sure." I reluctantly nodded. It felt like too much to keep this between us. Everything was just…too much. "I hate the thought of having this in my possession. What if someone finds it and thinks I stole it?"

"Would you like me to hold onto it?"

I hesitated only a moment, then nodded. "Yes, please." I handed her the necklace.

"I'll tuck it away where no one can find it. Then, once we have enough information that they'll believe us, we'll take it to Declan, then to the police."

I nodded as a weight lifted from my shoulders. I no longer had to bear the burden alone. Everything would be fine now. It would all be over soon.

Chapter Fourteen

That evening before dinner, I worked on my book for a few hours. I hadn't yet told Jillian that I was changing the premise to back up the paranormal things we'd always scoffed at. Regardless of whether she wanted the book once she learned about the changes, I had to write it. Some force was compelling me, some inner demon that needed exorcising by way of the book. Maybe I just needed to tell Eleanor's story.

I stood and stretched, and my feet took me to the window as they often did. I pulled the curtain aside and stared into the darkness. What was with the people in this house? Did any of them wish Eleanor harm? Declan…could he really have murdered his own sister? Or anyone, for that matter. While I knew him to be somewhat cold and standoffish, I'd also seen glimpses of tenderness.

I let out a long sigh and dropped the curtain, then stepped back. Dinner was more than an hour away. I needed a walk to clear my head.

I went downstairs and grabbed my winter gear from the front closet and slipped it on, then went outside.

I shoved my hands into my pockets. When would we have enough to go to the authorities with the pendant? Really, there was nothing more we could do. I mean, I couldn't just go around asking people, *hey, do you know how this was ripped from Eleanor's neck and ended up in the woods at Spring River? Because, if you do, I assume you're the one who did it...therefore, the one who killed her.*

Right, that would be smart.

An almost electric sensation in the air pulled me from my thoughts. I lifted my head to see Eleanor. She was waiting. I knew what it meant.

I walked in her direction and, as was our custom, she stayed six feet in front of me, and I followed obediently. We took the path that led to the carriage house...and to her grave. I shuddered as the full realization settled on me. I was following, seeing, believing in, a dead woman. Her earthly body was buried nearby, yet here she was...or at least some form of her. With a modicum of ability to think, to feel. Otherwise, why would she be so determined for me to find the truth? If indeed, that was her goal. Maybe she was a prankster, and she was messing with my head. But I didn't believe that. There was definitely a secret to be discovered.

The wind picked up as we walked, and I began to question my decision. Following a ghost out into the woods in subzero temperatures, where she might have actually been murdered, was not wise. But I was in too deep. I had to find out what happened to her. Not only for justice, but for my sanity.

She took the right fork in the path, the one leading to the carriage house. Although it was futile to go there—since I was unable to gain access—I was immeasurably relieved that she chose the carriage house instead of her grave. I was freaked out about the thought of visiting her grave *with* her.

I halted outside the carriage house doors. "Okay, we're here, Eleanor. What now?"

She hovered in that waiting way she had. I tried the doors. They were as firmly shut as before. I walked around to the sides, the back, trying each window and the rear door. My gloved hands were soaked by the time I'd tried them all, and I was freezing. Darkness had fallen. Wind moaned in the trees above my head.

"Okay, I'm done. I have no idea what I'm doing out here, but—"

My words were cut off as I was grabbed from behind. A strong arm slid around me and pinned my arms to my sides. I jerked wildly but was unable to free myself. I tried to turn my head, and a hand clamped over my mouth. I scrambled in my pocket for the mace.

A low voice bit out, "Where is it?" The hand eased off my mouth. "If you scream, I'll kill you. Tell me where it is."

I panted, trying to catch my breath but only managed to breathe in wind that froze my lungs. "What? I don't know what you're—"

An arm tightened around me and gripped me under the chin. Rough canvas gloves abraded my flesh. "Don't play games with me. I overheard you. You have it. I know you do."

I tried to identify the voice, but the man—I was sure based on the strength and low voice, that it was a man—was speaking in a harsh whisper. Maybe purposely disguising his voice? And he hadn't let me see his face. That meant he might not kill me. I tried to focus on that thought rather than the fear choking me.

Before I could speak again, a sound caught my attention. Footsteps crashing over the icy ground.

Someone else was coming.

My assailant must have heard it too. He shoved me, hard, and I landed in the freezing snow, my head slamming against the side of the carriage house. Pain spiked through my skull and down through my shoulders, and I cried out. A wave of darkness closed over me. I squeezed my eyes shut, fighting against the blackness. I couldn't pass out. I didn't know where the man had gone. Or what new danger was upon me.

"Camille?" Hands touched my shoulders, lifting me gently from the cold ground. The voice sounded like…Declan. But he would never be this kind. "What happened? Are you okay?"

Fingers lightly brushed the hair from my face, but they touched the place where I'd hit my head, and I winced, then opened my eyes. Declan's lovely gray eyes stared into mine. I almost wept with relief.

"Declan?" My voice was a hoarse whisper.

"Come on, you're bleeding. Let's get you inside. Can you walk?"

I nodded. The movement hurt, and I winced. Nausea rose to my throat, but I swallowed it back. Even in my dazed state, I knew I didn't want to be sick in front of Declan.

He wrapped his arm around my shoulder and guided me to the carriage house doors. "Hang onto me. I'll get you out of this weather."

My mind registered surprise as he unlocked the door and pushed it open. He was allowing me access to the top-secret carriage house. Maybe that meant he'd have to kill me. A giggle escaped, and Declan's worried gaze swept over my face, but he didn't speak.

A smell of mustiness and some other more pungent

odor greeted me. Was that…paint? I blinked in the dusty gloom. Declan gingerly lowered me to a chair and knelt in front of me, his face was only inches from mine. He ripped a strip of cloth off the shirt he wore beneath his coat and pressed it to my forehead.

His expression was solemn. "What happened out there? Did someone do this to you?"

"Ye-yes. I don't know who it was. I couldn't see him, and I didn't recognize his voice. But, a man grabbed me and…"

A dark cloud of anger came over his face. He stood abruptly. "Stay here. I'll lock you in."

"Wait, Declan?" I didn't know what I was going to say, but it didn't matter, because he was already out the door.

I shivered, partly from cold and partly from the aftermath of the attack. Who the hell was he? The killer, no doubt. But who? Why couldn't I recognize his voice, or have gotten a glimpse of him? And, what had he wanted? What did he think I had hidden?

I wasn't sure how much time had passed, but the door opened and Declan stomped in. He wore a thunderous scowl. "Not a sign. I followed footprints for several yards, but they disappeared into the woods. Dammit." He stalked over to where I still sat. "You have no idea who it was?"

I shook my head, then flinched at the pain it caused. "Not a clue."

"You mentioned his voice, so he said something to you. What did he say?"

How much to tell him? I wasn't ready to bring up the necklace, and definitely not his sister's ghost. "He asked me where 'it' was."

"It what?"

"I have no idea. He seemed to think I knew. But I swear, I didn't." And while I *was* keeping secrets from Declan, that much was true. I didn't know what he wanted.

"Damn," he bit out.

I stood. A wave of dizziness overtook me, and I closed my eyes.

"Are you okay?" I felt his hands land on my shoulders, and my eyes flew open.

I stepped back. "I'm fine. Just a little dizzy."

My eyes had adjusted to the gloom, and I could see more clearly now. I stared past him, taking in items I hadn't noticed before. Paintings. Several paintings stacked all over the floors, on a bench, a few on easels. I squinted, trying to see them more clearly. When I did, I gasped.

The one closest to me was a man's torso with bloody gore where the head should be. The figure held a lantern in one hand and a miner's helmet in the other. In another, a young man, tuxedo covered in blood, stared in horror at the blood-soaked bride at his feet.

I rose to my feet, holding the cloth to my wound. I couldn't take my gaze off the images. "My God." My mouth was dry, my heart beating like mad. "What…what is this?"

Declan's expression was grim. "These are my sister's. She was obsessed with the spook light. She spent hours upon hours in here creating these macabre paintings."

I walked slowly around, eyeing each painting with a morbid fascination. I stopped in front of one depicting a young Indian maiden and a brave, hands clasped together, bodies broken and lying on stones in a shallow pool of water "Why are you keeping them hidden in here?"

"I didn't want others to see, to know how far her mind had deteriorated. She worked so hard to gain respect and re-establish an upstanding reputation in the community. After she died, I didn't want people to know about this side of her. I wanted to keep the ground she'd gained intact." His voice was pain-filled, forlorn. My heart squeezed in sympathy. This was not the attitude, nor were those the words of a man who had killed his sister. Declan was innocent, I knew it deep in my soul.

I moved closer to him and rested my hand on his bicep. His flesh was warm against my freezing skin. A trill of delight at the contact swept through me, catching me off guard. Flustered, I released him and stepped back. "I-I'm so terribly sorry. For what you both must have suffered."

He nodded, then frowned. "You're freezing."

I hadn't realized it, but I was shivering. My clothes were soaked from where I'd fallen in the snow. My teeth chattered uncontrollably.

"Here." He peeled my coat off me and dropped it to the floor. He took his off and wrapped it around my shoulders. The lining was still warm from his body, and it smelled like him. A fresh, piney, masculine scent— not cologne, most likely the soap he used. Declan didn't seem like a man who would wear cologne. He was a throwback, a man's man.

He pulled the edges of his coat together at my breasts and simultaneously tugged me closer. I didn't know if it was intentional, but neither of us moved away. Heat flamed between our bodies. I drew in a shaky breath, my eyes locked on his, and moved a smidgen nearer.

The room became still. The air sizzled, heavy with tension. Silence fell, the sounds of the wind and snow outside seeming magnified.

"Camille?" His voice came out uneven. The word was a plea and a prayer at the same time. His hands slipped from the coat to my shoulders, becoming a caress through the thick material.

"Yes," I whispered. A statement, not a question.

He let out a breath as if in capitulation and tipped his head forward, fusing his lips to mine. My knees wobbled, and I gave a little whimper. The cloth I'd been using for my head dropped to the ground, but I barely noticed. My mind whirled with amazement. This was *real*. Declan Rush, impenetrable man of steel, was holding me in his arms, his mouth doing delicious things, his tongue dancing against mine. Lance had never kissed me like this. No one in the *universe* had ever been kissed like this. My skin ignited with electrical sparks, and heat exploded inside me.

Chapter Fifteen

Declan broke away with a groan and stared down at me. His chest rose as he took in long, slow breaths. "I'm sorry, Camille. That was uncalled for."

I swallowed the knot in my throat and nodded. When I could speak, I said, "It's okay. We both lost our heads for a moment." I cringed, and my gaze wandered to the headless miner. I didn't know whether to laugh or cry. What kind of insanity had I gotten myself involved in? Not only was I being harassed by a ghost who had apparently been murdered and wanted me to expose her killer, I was falling for a man who had the emotions of a droid and lived fifteen hundred miles away. *Nice, Cami.* I stepped away. "We probably should get to the house and call the police." I started to shrug out of his coat. "Here."

He pulled it back up around my shoulders. "No, you keep this on. Yours is soaked."

"But you'll freeze out there."

"I'll be fine. Come on, let's go."

He snatched my coat up from the floor, and I followed him out of the carriage house. He hunched his shoulders against the cold but didn't complain.

Misery and confusion attached to me as I walked alongside him in silence. What had the kiss meant? This time, we'd both been sober. Had he just given in to a momentary impulse or did he have feelings for me too?

207

I inwardly scoffed. Not likely. He barely knew me, and I had done nothing in our interactions so far to impress him. He looked at me as a bundle of trouble, I was certain. Shaking up his calm, quiet, reclusive life. He'd no doubt be immensely relieved when I left. The realization was oddly depressing. Both that I would be leaving soon, and that Declan would be relieved.

****

The next morning, I slept in. Declan and I had been up late speaking with the police about my attack. They said they'd take a look around, but with no more information than I gave them, they didn't seem hopeful they'd find the guy. I had to agree.

My head still throbbed, and the injury had left a mark, but it appeared I would live. I skipped breakfast but poured a cup of coffee in the empty kitchen, then went to the library and called Jillian. She answered with, "How is the book coming? Are you calling to tell me it's done?"

I bit my lip. "Not exactly."

"Then what? You're not stalled, are you?"

"Uh…not exactly."

"For God's sake, spit it out." Her impatient editor voice was in full play.

I plunged in the deep end. "What would you think about going a different direction?"

"Such as?"

How much to tell her? I couldn't say I'd been semi-communicating with a ghost. That would be too much. And, in spite of my interaction, I wasn't quite sure I believed it myself. "I think there might be something to this spook light thing. I thought I could change courses and write about how real the phenomenon is."

A gasping, choking sound came over the line. "Don't say things like that when I'm taking a drink of hot coffee. I nearly choked to death." I waited while she took a couple of dramatic breaths. "Okay. Better. Now is the time you tell me you aren't serious."

"But I am serious. The light is real." I hesitated, then blurted, "I saw it."

A few moments of silence passed. "Okay, you saw a light. Was it a streetlight, a car light, the moon, perhaps? Please don't tell me you believe it was some inexplicable *ghost* light?"

"But...I do believe that. I really do."

"Oh dear God, Cami. You're my cynic, my myth busting queen. How the hell can you turn on me?"

"Because I saw it. Truly. And it's not like anything I've ever seen." Well, other than Eleanor's ghost, which was much more startling, but I'd already blown her mind with the light, I wasn't going to add a ghost in the mix. "I promise, there is something otherworldly about it. I have pictures and everything. Please, let me send you a few chapters of my revisions so I can show you where I'm going with the book. If you hate it, I'll go back to our original plan." Although, how I could now that I didn't believe my own debunking, I wasn't sure. But I was under contract; I had to give her something. Hopefully, she would like my *new* something.

She let out a long—extremely long—sigh. "Okay, fine. But with no internet in that godforsaken wilderness, how do you intend to send me the chapters?"

"I'll get someone to take me into town. To the library." But it was the weekend, and the library was closed. "I can't send them until Monday." That would also give me time to actually write them.

"Okay, fine. I'll wait until Monday. But they'd better knock my socks off."

"They will, promise."

"Cool. Because I'm about to knock your socks off."

"Oh?"

"Have you spoken with Lance or Kathleen?"

"God, no. Not only do I not have cell service, and not only do we have this really awkward wedge between us, they're on their honeymoon. Of course I haven't spoken with them."

"Well, that's just it." Her voice was filled with excitement and a touch of smugness, like she couldn't wait to drop a bombshell on me. "They aren't on their honeymoon. Want to know why? Ask me why."

"Okay, why?"

"Because..." She let the word hang between us for a moment. Irritation pricked at me. Normally, I enjoyed her bent for the dramatic, but now, it was just pissing me off. "Because, they didn't get married!"

Shock rendered me silent for a few seconds. "They...what? Why not?"

"Lance called it off. I'm not sure why, but Kathleen was crushed. How great is that? Karma, am I right?"

Somehow, the news didn't fill me with the same delight it did Jillian. I evaluated my emotion and realized that rather than relief or hope or satisfaction, I felt a little...sad. For my sister. She must be broken-hearted. "That's awful."

"Awful? They got what they deserved. Misery."

"No, I mean, I feel bad for Kathleen. I know she must love him a great deal. She wouldn't have been with him otherwise. Wouldn't have been with the man I was going to marry unless she really loved him."

"Are you kidding me right now? Your sister betrayed you, stabbed you in the back. And, what if Lance called it off because of you? What if he realized he still loves you? I mean, not that I want you back together with that asshole, but wouldn't it be great if that's what he wanted? So you could dump *his* ass?"

No. It wasn't what I wanted. The thought of Lance available, perhaps still in love with me, did absolutely nothing for me. I truly, thoroughly, honestly didn't care. Geez. I must not have really been in love with him or I wouldn't be over it this quickly. My sister did me a favor. I couldn't explain all this to Jillian. She wouldn't understand. Hell, I didn't understand myself. An image of Declan arose, his intense gray eyes glittering with the rare tenderness I'd glimpsed a few times. A tenderness I wanted to see again. Directed toward me...

Oh, no...

I was anxious to end the call. I couldn't focus on our conversation with that new and unnerving revelation pecking at my brain. "Listen, I need to go. Someone's waiting for the phone."

"Okay, sure. I'm sorry. I thought you'd be happier at my news."

"You know, I would have thought so too. If you see Kathleen, would you tell her I'm sorry and when I get back, I want to see her?"

"If you insist." Reluctance and disapproval colored her tone. "Get those Chapters to me Monday. If I love them, we'll talk about changing courses."

"You'll love them." I hung up before she could argue.

A few hours, later, I went into the kitchen in search of lunch, my mind still turning over Jillian's news. Why didn't I feel at least a modicum of vindication?

Jean greeted me with her usual cheeriness. I had lunch with Jin and Roxanne, who were checking out that day and going back home. They looked at one another as if they were even more in love than they had been when they arrived. Was it possible such love did exist? They seemed to have found it. Would I ever get that lucky?

****

I couldn't sleep that night. I worked on my chapters until well into the night and churned out the best writing I'd ever done in my life. I was determined to convince Jillian to let me publish this version of the spook light story. It was real, and there was no logical explanation for it. The words flew.

I'd written until three a.m. And my back and fingers were cramping. The seat in the alcove was plush, but after four hours, no position was comfortable.

I lifted my laptop and stood. Sharp tingles moved through my legs where they'd fallen asleep. I gingerly walked across the room until my limbs felt normal again, then I threw a robe on over my nightshirt and headed downstairs.

The light in the kitchen was on, and a pot was boiling on the stove, steam hissing from it. The stench of scorched milk assailed me. Jean would never leave a pot cooking like that. But she was the only one I knew of in the house who warmed milk in the middle of the night, definitely the only one who wouldn't have used a microwave. I looked around but saw no one.

Hurrying to the stove to turn the flame off before the house caught on fire. I rounded the kitchen island and halted, a scream strangling my throat. A person lay on the floor, just in front of the stove where the pot still hissed. A woman…her legs sticking out at an odd angle beneath the floral robe. Her face was away from me, but I didn't have to see it to know.

Chapter Sixteen

I dropped to my knees beside her. "Jean?" I shook her shoulder. "Jean? Please, wake up."

Her head rolled back, and I stumbled away, losing my balance and crashing my head into the oven. She wasn't going to wake up. Not ever.

Her eyes were wide. Blood seeped from a red gash across her neck. This time, the scream came. I shot to my feet and covered my mouth, sobs trying to burst past my trembling fingers.

I skirted Jean's body and took off at a run toward the library…to the phone. Although I knew in my soul, she was beyond help, I had to call, had to try.

As I flew through the darkness of the living room, I ran headlong into a solid object. A person. I jumped back and yelped. The killer. Whoever killed Jean was here. Now he would kill me. I whirled to run, not even looking at the face of the man. I had to get away, had to find help…

"Camille! Stop, Camille! It's me, Declan."

I paused but didn't turn around. Declan…he could be the killer.

"Camille? What's wrong?"

He'd reached me now, and he gently took my shoulders and turned me to face him. "For God's sake, you're shaking. What happened?"

I looked up at him and opened my mouth, but my

lips trembled so badly I couldn't speak.

He drew me into his body. "Shhhh, it's okay. I'm here now. Everything is okay."

I shook my head against his chest, wanting to nuzzle in and stay there. But I couldn't. I pulled back. "I-it's not okay. Jean...she..." A shudder ripped through me. "She's dead."

His face blanched. "What? What are you talking about?"

"Call 9-1-1. Please. Hurry."

"Show me."

"There's no time, she needs help. Please." I rushed past him into the library grabbed the phone, punching in 9-1-1. In halting, trembling words, I told the operator what had happened, what I'd found.

Declan's eyes widened as he listened. "No...God."

When I hung up, I took his hand and led him to the kitchen. He knelt down beside Jean. He placed a finger to the side of her neck, even though there was barely any neck left.

He sat back on his haunches and dropped his head. "Oh, God."

****

Loretta let in the sheriff—a thin man with a worn face and kind eyes. He shook hands with Declan and turned to me. "I'm Sheriff Ford. You must be the young lady who found Ms. Hibbert."

I wrapped my arms around my body and nodded.

"We'll get some crime scene techs out here shortly. In the meantime, I'd like to speak with you and Mr. Rush. Alone."

"I'll make coffee—" Loretta halted, probably remembering what was in the kitchen. "I'll leave you to talk." She hurried from the room, her head bent, hand to her mouth.

I sat, and Declan settled on the sofa next to me. I had the strangest urge to reach out and take his hand, for comfort, for strength. But that wouldn't be received very well, and it might raise questions with the sheriff that I had no answers to.

Sheriff Ford took out a notepad and pen. "Okay, take me through it. From the very beginning. Where had you been? Why were you in the kitchen at three a.m.?"

I told him everything.

"Did you see anyone else in the kitchen?"

"No, there was no one there by the time I arrived." My voice cracked. "Only Jean."

"Did you hear anything? Like maybe a door closing when the intruder left?"

I shook my head. "I think he'd already been gone a while when I arrived."

"Why is that?"

"The milk had been boiling several minutes. It was scorched and all boiled out."

"That doesn't mean he'd just left."

I sat for a moment, gathering my thoughts. "I'm thinking that he probably didn't even notice the milk simmering on the stove, meaning she'd probably just put it on." I looked up at the sheriff. "If he'd noticed the pot boiling, surely he would have turned it off so as not to draw attention to…Jean…and what he'd done for as long as possible."

A light of respect came into the sheriff's eyes. "You might be right." He made a few notes in the pad and looked at Declan. "Where were you?"

"I was reading in the library. Then I heard Ms. Burditt screaming. I came out to investigate, and she ran into me. Literally, slammed into me, she was running so hard."

My cheeks heated. "I didn't see him. I was trying to get to the phone."

Sheriff Ford nodded and said to Declan, "Did you see anyone else?"

"Not a soul."

His words sent a shiver over my spine. Not a soul... not even the soul of his sister who was haunting the inn. And now, there had been another death.

"Was Ms. Hibbert in the habit of making milk in the middle of the night?"

"Yes," Declan and I spoke simultaneously, then shot a look at one another.

"I'm sorry," I added. "I've only known Jean for just over a week, but in the time I've been here, I've found her making warm milk in the middle of the night a few times."

Declan said, "My housekeeper had arthritis. It kept her from sleeping well. The warm milk helped her to rest."

My heart ached. I didn't know she had arthritis. She was in all that pain and still worked and served others.

"Do you know anyone who would want to hurt her?"

"No," we said together again.

But, it occurred to me that I did know something that might be related. My stomach tightened with guilt. This could be my fault.

"Actually," I put in. "I have a bit of information

that might have something to do with what happened."

The sheriff and Declan both looked at me questioningly.

"Yes?" Sheriff Ford prompted.

"I—I found a necklace. In the trees at Spring River a few nights ago. I showed it to Jean, and she suggested we not say anything until we knew more about what was going on. She offered to hold onto it for me."

"Why would a broken necklace have any significance?"

I drew in a long breath, gathering my courage. Declan would be incensed. "I—because. The necklace belonged to Eleanor Chaney."

"What?" Declan exploded. "What the hell are you talking about?"

I winced. "I found the Spinel pendant Eleanor always wore. It was several feet from where she…drowned. And it was broken."

Declan shot to his feet and towered over me. I scrunched back into the sofa cushion.

"And you didn't feel the need to tell me?"

The sheriff spoke. "Okay, settle down, Declan. Let's talk this through like civilized people and get to the bottom of it."

Declan's fists clenched, and he stepped back. He remained standing a few feet away. I couldn't look at him, but I could feel his glower.

The sheriff pursed his lips. "You found a piece of jewelry belonging to Eleanor, and you didn't take it to the authorities?"

I sat forward, feeling like the biggest fool in the world. "I was going to. I wanted to, but Jean talked me out of it. She had her suspicions that someone might have…killed Eleanor. She thought the necklace was a clue, but she said we should have more evidence before we took it to the authorities. I felt funny about holding onto it, so she said she would. She made me promise not to tell." I shot Declan a look, realizing my words sounded almost pleading. His stony expression didn't relax.

"You said the necklace was broken, and it was found a distance away from where she drowned? How do you know the location where she drowned?"

"I pieced it together from what Jean told me and what I read in the newspaper, at least the general vicinity. Besides, the necklace was twenty feet into the woods, nowhere near the water."

A growl left Declan's throat. "Son of a bitch."

The sheriff frowned. "So, you're saying…"

"I'm saying that she must have struggled with someone, in the trees. And that person dragged her to the water and killed her. Maybe he killed her in the woods and threw her in the water to make it look like an accident." Declan's swift intake of breath made me regret my directness. This was his sister I was talking about.

"No," the sheriff said. "Her lungs were filled with water. She definitely drowned."

I bit my lip and nodded slowly. "Then they struggled. And her necklace was broken in the scuffle. He dragged her to the water and drowned her."

The sheriff pursed his lips. "How are you so sure it's Eleanor's necklace? Even so, couldn't it have been lost another time?"

I shook my head. "It's a special necklace, a custom made Spinel that's been in her family for years. She wore it all the time." I took a deep breath. "She was wearing it the day she disappeared. Jean confirmed it. I'm sure that's why he wanted it."

"You keep saying 'he.' Assuming Eleanor was murdered, and regarding the person who did this to Jean, why are you so sure it's a man?"

I shoved a hand through my hair. "Because. He— or someone—a man—attacked me too."

The sheriff frowned. "What? When?"

I told him about the incident at the carriage house. "We called the police. One of your deputies came out."

"I'll check on the report. I must have been off that night." His gaze rested on my forehead where the injury now just looked like a series of scrapes and scratches. "Is that what happened to your head?"

I nodded. "But I'm fine now." Jean…not so much. My lip trembled. My chest tightened with grief, and sobs shook my shoulders as tears ran down my face. "Oh, God. The necklace, the attack. This is all my fault."

He sat forward and patted my knee. "There, there. Don't blame yourself."

But I couldn't help it. The man had wanted something from me. Was it the pendant? He'd figured out Jean had it. Had he found it? I had no idea where she'd hidden it. But I had a horrible feeling that she'd died protecting it.

Chapter Seventeen

The sheriff and crime scene techs left at six a.m. They didn't mention whether they'd found the necklace. Made sense. They'd want to keep it quiet until they'd solved the case. I was more exhausted and drained than I'd ever been in my life. Once the door closed behind them, Declan stalked away.

"Wait," I called out.

He halted, his shoulders set in tight lines, but didn't turn around.

He was angry. I understood. I'd kept something from him related to his sister's death. How could he ever forgive me?

"I know you're mad," I said to his back. "But I was only doing it to protect you. I wanted to know more before I brought you into it and upset you for no reason."

He turned. His expression was ravaged, his face lined with anger, grief, and fatigue. "Upset me? How upset do you think I am now, Ms. Burditt? Can you venture a guess?"

"I know, but—"

He brought up a hand to silence me. "Next time, don't decide for yourself what's good for me. Let me be the judge of that."

I nodded miserably. He turned, furious strides taking him toward his quarters. Wearily, I climbed the stairs and fell into bed. Even though I'd been up all night, I didn't sleep well. Each time I closed my eyes, I saw poor, sweet Jean's dead body. And, the disgust in Declan's gaze.

****

Once I finally fell asleep, I slept most of the day. It was nearly five in the evening when I got up. Funny, I didn't feel all that rested.

I went downstairs to find Loretta in the sitting room. Her eyes were red, her cheeks splotchy. She was hanging up the phone, and she looked up and saw me. She gave a small, sad smile. "That was Jean's daughter, up in St. Louis. She's making arrangements to have Jean's body taken there. The family is from here, but Jean is the only one left in the area. Shannon wants her mother buried near her."

"I'm sorry," I said softly. "I'm sure you've known Jean a very long time."

Loretta sniffed and nodded. "Yes, for years. She was the one who referred me for the job after Eleanor—" her face paled. "Now, both of them. Dead…"

"Yes. So sad."

"I hear they're re-opening Eleanor's case. That maybe her death wasn't an accident."

"Is that right?" Good. Now, I could stop playing amateur detective. Eleanor hadn't made an appearance in the last few days. Maybe she realized I'd be no help. I'd accomplished nothing, other than putting Jean in danger. Once again, guilt gripped my heart. It did no good to tell myself it was Jean's idea to keep the necklace secret, that she insisted on holding onto it. I should have told someone else. Now Jean was dead, and Declan hated me. Even Eleanor had abandoned me.

I watched her closely for any hint of concern or guilt. I found none. But that didn't mean she wasn't involved. She might just not have a conscience about it. But then, the person who attacked me was a man...

I was tired of thinking about it, tired of trying to find answers to questions that had none.

Loretta studied me intently. "Haven't you heard anything about it? Did the police mention Eleanor to you when they questioned you?"

"No, why would they? She died months before I came here." I played dumb. I wasn't sure how much Declan had told her. I wasn't sure how close the two of them were. He seemed to look upon her as no more than an employee, but there were times I thought she had feelings for him that went beyond the working relationship. But then, what did I know? I didn't even pick up on the fact that my sister and fiancé were hot for each other.

"Right. But if the two cases are connected. And since you're the one who discovered Jean...I don't know. I just wondered."

"No. I'm sure whatever they know about Eleanor's death—and Jean's for that matter—they'll keep quiet so as not to hamper the investigation."

"I hope they find him." She wrapped her arms around herself and visibly shuddered. "And soon. I mean, if he's killed twice, he could kill again."

Yes, he could kill again. And since he'd already come after me, would I be next? It might depend on whether he'd found the necklace. If that was what he wanted from me, and he'd gotten it when he killed Jean, maybe he was done. Maybe the rest of us were safe. Although, in this big, spooky house, with only myself,

Declan, Holt, Troy, and Loretta, I didn't feel safe at all. Especially since I had the floor all to myself now that the Kangs were gone. Maybe I should leave, too. Check out early and forget the research. I could finish the book on what I had so far. I wasn't due to check out for three more days. I'd paid the room in full. It wasn't like I'd be cheating the inn.

Having made my decision, I felt an odd mixture of relief and regret. When I left here, I would never see Declan again. And while that shouldn't bother me, it did. Deeply. I'd never felt as alive with Lance as I did in the short time I'd known Declan. Our interaction had been tainted by mystery, murder, sorrow, and mistrust, but it had given me more pleasure and confidence than I'd ever had. But that was all over now. I had to put it behind me. Leaving was the right thing to do…for me.

I should check with the sheriff's office, make sure they didn't need me for anything before I left. And I'd have to call the airlines. But if I got the all clear, I would leave as soon as possible. I could finish my book in Miami, and if Jillian didn't like the new chapters, I'd fake it and write as we'd originally planned. After all, my entire life seemed to hinge on secrets and deception. What would a few more lies matter?

****

Later that evening, Loretta called my room to let me know I had a phone call. Assuming it was Jillian, I hurried downstairs to the phone.

My body tensed when Lance's voice came over the line. "God, Cami. I'm so glad I finally reached you."

"Why have you been trying to reach me?" I kept my tone cold, disinterested. Which I discovered wasn't that difficult. Hearing his voice did absolutely nothing for me—other than annoy.

"I wanted to tell you…I ended things with Kathleen."

"Yes, I'm aware."

"Are you aware of why?" His voice had lowered in what I assumed was supposed to be a seductive tone. It wasn't. "It's because of you. I was a fool. I don't know what I was thinking. I just…the thing with Kathleen was exciting and new. You and I have been together so long…"

"And you became bored."

"Exactly!" As if realizing how that sounded, he rushed on, "But I didn't appreciate what I had. What *we* had. I couldn't marry Kathleen. You're the one I want. The only one I want. When will you be back?"

"It doesn't matter."

"Sure it does, I want to see you, so I need to know when you'll be home."

"No, I mean, this, you, your feelings. They don't matter, and I don't want to see you when I return."

Silence pulsed in my ear. Then he said, "What? You can't mean that." He gave a disbelieving chuckle. "You were devastated when I ended things. There's no way you can be over me this quickly. You just want to punish me, and I understand—"

"No you don't." I cut him off. "You don't understand a damn thing. I *am* over you. Maybe because I never really loved you in the first place. And right now, all I am where you're concerned is pissed that you hurt my sister. So…goodbye, Lance. Don't call me again."

"Cami, please, you can't—"

But I could. And I did. I slammed the phone into

the cradle with a profound satisfaction that would have been missing with a cell phone.

Free…I was free of Lance and whatever feelings I'd had for him. Thank God.

Feeling as though a burden had been lifted, in spite of my lingering sadness over Jean, I went into the kitchen where I found Loretta making a chicken spinach salad.

She looked up. "I made enough for two. You hungry?"

Her offer surprised me. While she'd never been hostile, she hadn't been overly friendly either. Maybe she was feeling as alone as I was. "Yes, thanks."

The dinner was solemn, but tasty. Afterward, I went to my room to pack. I'd called the sheriff's office, and he agreed I could leave, as long as I left contact information. After all, I was a witness, not a suspect.

When I'd told Loretta over dinner I was checking out early, she hadn't seemed to care one way or another. It wasn't like we'd gotten close or anything. No one here would care that I was leaving. I paused in my packing as a pang shot through my gut. No one at home would care that I'd come back, either.

Self-pity surfaced and threatened to overtake me. I had friends, sure, but no close friends. Kathleen, my only family, didn't care about me. Jillian was a friend— of sorts—but she was first and foremost my editor. I could be murdered here, and no one would be all that affected. The thought was sobering…and depressing.

I vowed to change that when I returned home. I was twenty-five, not ninety-five. I had a lot of life ahead of me. I would get out more, take dance or scrapbooking lessons, join a book club, open myself up to new people, new possibilities. And forget I'd ever heard of Quapaw Oklahoma *or* Declan Rush.

Feeling slightly less despondent, I packed my suitcases. It was ten, but I had only been awake for five hours, and I was not even close to ready to go to bed. I had called Rita, the girl who'd driven me here, and she would pick me up tomorrow. My flight left at four in the afternoon.

I pulled out the Stephen King book and settled into the alcove. I'd already completed the chapters for Jillian and now, instead of emailing them from here, I could wait until I got home. To the land of internet and cell service and civilization.

I was more than halfway finished with the story, now completely drawn in. The intensity had increased. I was not only *reading* the story, I was in it, with the characters, and I didn't know how the hell we were going to get out of this mess. During a particularly harrowing scene, a loud crash sounded outside. I jumped and screamed, tossing the book to the floor.

Heart beating like crazy, I drew back the curtain and peeked out the window.

I sighed in relief. A large tree branch, laden with ice, lay on the ground below. *Damn*. Great timing. Nearly gave me a heart attack.

I rose from the window seat, trying to decide if I was brave enough to resume reading, when a filmy glow in my peripheral caught my attention. My pulse sped up, and I whirled to find Eleanor in the corner of the room. I was surprised to feel a measure of relief. She hadn't abandoned me after all.

Once she had my attention, she glided to the door. *Oh great*. Another adventure.

Now that the stakes were death, I was a bit reluctant to follow her. But I couldn't stop now. If she could lead me to something that solved Jean's murder—and maybe her own—I wasn't going to give up just yet.

I followed her down the stairs, grabbed my coat and boots from the hall closet and hurriedly donned them, then went out the front door.

She was already halfway across the yard. I walked briskly, keeping as close to her as I could. She moved quickly, which was fine with me. As cold as it was outside, I wasn't up for a leisurely stroll.

She once more took me to the path, and once more, veered to the right, toward the carriage house. "Okay, Eleanor," I said, my breath puffing out like thick smoke in front of me. "I know about your paintings. I'm not sure what else you can show me. If the answer is in the paintings, I'm afraid I haven't figured it out." She kept going, and I continued to follow, though I stopped talking. I needed to save my breath for the hike.

As expected, we ended up at the carriage house. "We're here, now what? I can't get in, and even if I could, I know what's there. I just don't know what, precisely, you want me to see."

Irritatingly, she didn't speak. She simply floated through the door until she was inside the carriage house. And I was still outside. Brilliant.

I stomped my boots against the frozen ground, partly to stay warm, and partly out of pique. With a frustrated sigh, I shoved on the carriage house door. Expecting to meet resistance, I stumbled inside when the door swung open. Unlocked? What the hell? Had Declan forgotten to lock it when we left? He had been concerned about getting me back to the house, about contacting the police. And anxious to flee after giving in to a moment of insanity with the kiss. It was possible he hadn't locked it.

Eleanor glided to the painting of the young Indian couple. I walked over and stood in front of it, eyeing it more thoroughly. The maiden lay at an awkward angle, blood pouring from her head, drenching her long black hair. The brave lay nearby, his face twisted in an agonized expression. Though crudely drawn—Eleanor was talented, but not all that skilled—the painting was also compelling, haunting. The inner torment of the artist showed through. And, based on this painting, Eleanor had harbored a great deal of torment.

I lifted my hands and let them drop. "I'm sorry. I don't see what you want me to see." I peered more closely, trying to decipher a message in the picture. Nothing came to me. I looked over my shoulder at Eleanor. "Please, give me some other clue. Some hint as to what I'm supposed to see." Although her features were not defined, I thought I saw frustration in her expression. She began moving slowly backward. I followed, skirting around the painting. "Are you going to show me something a little clearer? Some clue I can actually figure out this time?" I'd followed her half a dozen steps when she suddenly whirled and flew at me. I screamed and toppled backward, into the painting. The easel and I crashed to the floor. "What the hell!" My words tremored out of me. In all the dealings with Eleanor, she'd never been threatening. Was she going to kill me? Could ghosts kill? If they couldn't make contact with humans, how could they kill? But she no longer looked menacing anyway. She'd backed off and, as was her habit, was waiting.

I untangled myself from the painting and easel, trying to gain my footing, when I saw that the back of the painting had been torn. There was apparently a false layer of canvas. A sheet of paper stuck out. I looked up at Eleanor. "Was this what you wanted me to see?"

I climbed to my feet, bent over and withdrew the paper. I frowned. "A birth certificate?" The child's name was Tate Kellow. He was born in Tulsa, Oklahoma on September 1, 1988. To Victoria Carr and…Benjamin Rush. Declan's father. There had been another child? That was possible. I'd never asked Declan if Eleanor was his only sibling. But the mother's name wasn't Rush. So…not Declan and Eleanor's mother? Victoria Carr…the name sounded familiar. Victoria Carr, Victoria Carr. Where had I heard it?

The memory came back, and I froze in shock. The woman murdered by Declan and Eleanor's father. My hands shook. I had no idea what it meant, but it had to mean something. *Think…* Why would Eleanor have a birth certificate listing the woman her father had killed as the mother? The question was who was the child? Chills raced over my skin. Was it…Declan? Dear God. If his father had killed his mother, then it only made sense that he was the one committing the murders. Maybe Eleanor had stumbled onto it.

The birth date was September 1, 1988. Declan's birthday was in June, and he would turn thirty, so he was born in '86. Whoever this belonged to would be twenty-seven right now. Unless Declan lied about his age and birthday? But why would he do that? And, those who knew him; Loretta, Jean, Holt, Troy, would all know when his birthday was. So, who was this Tate

Kellow?

I was so engrossed in the birth certificate, I'd almost forgotten about Eleanor, and I half expected her to have disappeared by now. But she was still there. Her expression—if I could call it that, and maybe I could. I'd seemed to learn to read her moods—was satisfied. As if we were done.

"Eleanor, if you think this solved the mystery, you're insane." I flicked a quick glance around at the paintings. "No offense. But, now I'm more confused. Who the hell is Tate Kellow?"

"It's me." A male voice spoke from the doorway.

Chapter Eighteen

I yelped, slapping the birth certificate to my chest, and squinted into the gloom. The figure walked toward me. I could see the outline of his shape but couldn't make out his features. But the voice…I recognized the voice. At the same moment realization dawned, he stepped closer, and I could see him clearly. Troy.

I instinctively shoved the birth certificate behind my back. "Troy? What are you doing here?" My voice shook more than I would have liked. I thought if I pretended I hadn't heard him say 'it's me' and didn't see the gun he held, he might believe that I believed this was just some innocent coincidence. *Ha, right…*

"You know exactly what I'm doing here. Give it to me." He motioned with his hand and glanced behind me.

"Give what to you?"

He chuckled and shook his head. "Don't play dumb. I know you're hiding my birth certificate behind your back. I heard you talking about it." He frowned. "Oddly, to Eleanor. Which is kind of creepy if you ask me. Why are you talking to a dead woman that you didn't even know?"

I looked out of the corner of my eye. Eleanor was no longer with us. Not that it would have mattered. She could do nothing for me. Ghosts apparently couldn't touch objects, couldn't move objects in spite of the lore.

If she could, she would have just knocked the painting off herself. Instead, she had to frighten me until I stumbled into it. I don't think scaring me until I stumbled into Troy would help much here. Her absence left me feeling even more alone, even though she would have been no help at all.

I brought the birth certificate from behind my back and held it out to him. He snatched it from me, moving way closer with the gun than I was comfortable with.

He stared down at it, still holding the gun on me. His mouth was drawn in a sad frown. "The bitch."

"Your mother?" I ventured a guess.

His head jerked up, and venom shot from his blue eyes. "No! Not my mother, she was a saint. That bitch, Eleanor. She tried to ruin everything."

I didn't want to enrage him further, but I had to stall for time until I figured something out. Maybe if I kept him talking, he'd forget he wanted to kill me. "What did she do? How did she ruin everything?"

He smirked. "Oh no, you're not going to distract me by getting me to pour my heart out. What you *are* going to do, is tell me where the necklace is."

"Necklace?"

He shot forward and grabbed my arm, jerked me to him and held the gun to my chin. "Yes, necklace, dammit. Don't pretend you don't know what I'm talking about. I know you gave the necklace to Jean. I heard you two talking about the argument between Holt and Eleanor. At first, I thought she was talking about my argument with Eleanor."

So, I *had* heard someone outside the kitchen that day. Troy had been listening to us.

"Just in case she knew something about me, I

bugged the kitchen. After I grabbed you at the carriage house, thinking you had the necklace, I listened to the recording. You gave it to her for safekeeping. But I know you know where it is. She wouldn't give it to me either, and you saw how that worked out for her."

So, he hadn't found it. Did that mean the police had it? Or had Jean hidden it so well even they hadn't found it? My only chance of stalling was to make him think I knew where it was. If he didn't think I could lead him to the necklace, he'd kill me.

"I'll tell you, if you promise not to hurt me."

A calculating gleam came into his eyes. "I don't want to hurt you, Cami. I like you. I just want to know where the necklace is. Not only is it worth a bundle, it's the only thing that can tie me to Eleanor, the only indicator her death was more than an accident, and I have to get my hands on it before the police do."

"So, you did kill her? Why? What happened between you two?"

He tut-tutted and shook his head like I was a wayward child. "Please, don't think you can distract me with conversation. Just give me the necklace, and I'll let you go."

"I don't believe you."

"Then why did you try to get me to promise, if you weren't going to believe me anyway?"

A gust of wind shuddered the windows, and he whipped his head around, relaxing his grip. I shoved against him, trying to knock the gun loose. It wobbled, but he tightened his hold and jammed it against my head.

My stomach roiled at the feel of his body so close to mine—this man was a sick, twisted killer. The odor of his sweat rose, increasing my nausea.

"Don't try anything stupid, or you'll get a bullet through your head. Jean held out on me, and I had to kill her. Don't make the same mistake. It's not worth your life. Just tell me where the damn necklace is."

"And then you'll kill me anyway." How could I not have realized Troy was the murderer? Eleanor had been leading me to him that day when I ran into Holt. I just hadn't clued in to it.

"I won't. I'm leaving as soon as I find the necklace. I've had my fill of this godforsaken place. All I want is to be free from here. I'll not get my share of the money now, but I won't leave empty handed. The necklace is all I want, Camille, I swear." He stepped away, still holding the gun on me.

I scrutinized the expression in his eyes. He seemed sincere. But then, he was a killer, so he wouldn't have any qualms about lying.

"Okay. I'll take you to it. But tell me about the birth certificate first, and why you killed Eleanor."

"No, no. You won't *take* me to it, you'll tell me where it is." Although his features were menacing, I was struck once more by his handsomeness. He resembled Declan, just a little, with those eyes, though his were blue while Declan's were silver gray. They had the same cleft in the chin, the same sensuous mouth...

Of course. "Declan's your brother. You killed your own sister?"

He frowned and narrowed his eyes on me. "I wouldn't have had to if the bitch had listened to reason."

"What reason? What did you want from her? Your

portion of the inn?"

"Enough!" He snarled. "No more chatting. Tell me where the necklace is now, or you die."

No more stalling. I was going to die…especially since I didn't even have the damn necklace.

Tears welled in my throat as cold, final fear washed through me. This was it. I was really going to die—

My terror turned to shock when the carriage house doors burst open. We both whirled to see Declan charging into the room.

"Oh, God…" I watched in horror as Troy brought the gun up and aimed at Declan's chest. I couldn't do anything. One move, and he might pull the trigger, whether he intended to or not.

Declan ignored Troy and turned his ravaged expression on me. "Camille, are you okay?"

I nodded, unable to speak.

Declan's eyes roamed over my body, as if making sure for himself that I spoke the truth. Then he turned his attention back to Troy. "What the hell is going on here?"

"Your girlfriend has something I need. Once I get it, I'll let the two of you go. Maybe you can talk her into cooperating."

"What does she have?"

I finally found my voice. "He wants Eleanor's necklace. The one I gave to Jean."

Declan frowned. "Why?"

"Because, genius, it's worth a fortune, and I need to get away. Far, far away. Before the cops find out."

"Find out what?" Declan's tone was as icy as the wind outside.

A sadistic smile curved Troy's lips. "That I killed her. Killed them both."

Declan flinched, and his gray eyes darkened with pain. It must have hurt deeply to hear someone speak so callously about murdering his sister. And I had once thought he could possibly have done it. What an idiot I'd been. Declan would never, ever hurt anyone. Not on purpose. And definitely not someone he loved.

I wanted to go to him, to put my arms around him and offer comfort, offer whatever he wanted from me. But a madman with a gun stood between us.

Troy motioned to me with the gun. "Get over here by your lover, so I can keep an eye on both of you."

I hurried to Declan's side, and he swept me up in a hug, holding me tightly to his body. He cupped the back of my head in his hands and kissed me firmly on the mouth. "God, I was so scared. When I came in and saw him holding a gun to you…"

I felt a shudder move through his large frame. In spite of the direness of our situation, a tremor of pleasant warmth coursed through my heart.

"You…care about me?"

He pulled back and looked into my face. "More than I ever thought possible."

"Well," Troy's harsh bark brought me back to reality. "As touching as this is, I'm going to have to cut it short. You know, I only need one of you alive to find the necklace." He pointed the gun at Declan's chest.

"No!" I threw myself in front of Declan. "If you kill him, you'll have to kill me too. And you'll never get what you want."

I had no idea, not an inkling of a plan, but I had to figure something out. Quickly.

"Then you'd better start talking, now."

Declan moved me aside and tucked me behind his body. "Don't hurt her. Let her go, and I'll get you the damned necklace."

"That's awfully self-sacrificing of you. I didn't know you had it in you." A smug smile came over his face. "Brother."

"Brother?" Declan repeated.

"Yes, that's right. I'm your brother. Your father's bastard. Although, he was the real bastard. I mean, after all, he did murder my mother."

"What?" Declan's voice was incredulous. "What the hell are you talking about?"

I stepped out from behind Declan and took hold of his hand. He seemed unaware of my presence until I spoke. "He has a birth certificate naming your father and Victoria Carr as the parents. The child's name is Tate Kellow. Troy claims that's his real name."

Declan shook his head. "That's not..." He shook it again. "That's not possible—"

Something behind Declan and me took Troy's focus. He stared past my shoulder. His eyes widened. A hoarse scream tore from his throat, and his face drained of all color. "What the—" He backed away, waving the gun wildly. "No, no, no."

I looked behind me, but I already knew what I'd see. Eleanor's spirit.

She hovered for a moment, then darted toward Troy. He lunged backward. "Stop! What are you? For God's sake, stop!" Another scream ripped from him, this one far from human.

Eleanor kept coming.

Declan stepped forward, and I moved as well,

although I'm not sure what either of us intended to do. Before we could do anything, Troy's panicky flight had him stumbling backward into a bench. He tripped. The gun went off. The side of his head exploded in a bloody mess, and he crumpled to the ground.

Eleanor loomed over him, then turned and seemed to stare at Declan and me for a few moments, and then she disappeared.

Chapter Nineteen

Declan knelt by his brother's body, his head bowed. "For God's sake. How could I not have known...how could he, how could Eleanor, have hidden this from me?"

I put my hand on his shoulder. "I don't know. "I'm sorry. So terribly sorry."

He nodded and placed his hand over mine. "I'm just glad you're okay." He stood and pulled me into his arms. "I don't know what I'd have done if anything happened to you."

I held onto him tightly. I wasn't sure what this meant...if he thought he cared about me, if I would ever see him again, but for now, I was content just to be warm—and safe—in his arms. "How did you know I was out here?" And, I wanted to add, did you see your sister's ghost, or was that just me...and obviously, Troy.

"Eleanor."

His response shocked me. I lifted my brows.

"Her ghost. She came to me. I couldn't believe my eyes. I thought I was losing my mind. But, she led me out here. To you."

"Wow." So, she'd helped me after all. Eleanor was apparently a more caring being in death than she had been in life.

"You saw her too, right? I'm not insane, am I? And

Troy…she scared him. He saw her too. That's why he freaked out."

"I saw her. And yes, he must have seen her as well."

I didn't tell him this wasn't the first time I'd seen her. There would be time later to explain what had led up to tonight. Right now, I was too weary, my mind too full of all that had taken place.

As if by unspoken agreement, we turned to head to the house. I was stepping over the torn canvas when I spotted the corner of a piece of paper stuck to the back. I bent to retrieve it.

"What's that?" Declan asked.

"I'm not sure." I unfolded it and discovered a letter, written in a neat, feminine hand. My eyes shot down to the bottom of the page. It was signed by Eleanor. "Here." I handed the paper to Declan. I'd inserted myself into his family, his life, enough. I would let him have this moment of privacy, the last words of his sister. If he wanted to share them with me, he would.

Declan read the letter silently, his eyes moving over the words, pain reflected in their silvery depths.

He didn't speak as we headed back to the main house. I was curious as to the contents of the letter, but I wouldn't pry. If he wanted me to know, he would tell me.

****

Hours later, Declan came in to the library where I sat, staring at a blank computer screen. I'd been willing myself to work on my book so I'd have something to occupy myself while I waited for the police to leave, but the words wouldn't come. My mind was mush. I was totally useless and would be until I spoke with Declan. Until I found out what was in the letter—if he wanted to share it with me. But mostly, until I found out where we stood. If there even was a 'we.'

He settled onto the sofa next to me, and I placed my laptop on the table.

"How are you?" I asked softly.

He gave a long, weary sigh and leaned back into the sofa cushion, pulling me with him, holding me against his chest, his chin resting on my head. "I'm reeling. I never…I just can't believe all that happened. Right under my nose."

"I'm sorry," I whispered.

His fingers gently stroked my hair. "The note from Eleanor was quite illuminating. She said that if the letter and birth certificate were found, it meant she was dead. And that Tate Kellow had killed her."

I wanted to prod him for details, but I waited patiently. Even though the topic was horrific and tragic, the rumble of his words from the warm chest beneath my ear was comforting, pleasurable even. I could have stayed like that for eternity.

"Troy—Tate, was my father's illegitimate child. His mother, Victoria, confronted my father, demanded he acknowledge his son. My father killed her. Tate learned about it and formulated a plan to obtain his share of the family fortune. Eleanor didn't trust him. Of course, she didn't trust anyone. She was going through his things and discovered the birth certificate. She confronted him and insisted he leave, or she'd destroy him."

"My God. All of this without mentioning a word to you."

He nodded grimly. "She probably assumed I wouldn't go along with her plan. That I would have wanted to get to know him. She didn't want to share our inheritance with me, so she damned sure wasn't going to share with a stranger." He let out a humorless laugh. "She gave him enough money to set up somewhere new but assured him he would never have access to any of the Rush money. I'm not sure how he caught up to her at Spring River. She might have been taking one of her walks, or she could have been planning a swim, although it doesn't appear she had a bathing suit with her. Regardless, somehow, they encountered one another. I would imagine they fought."

"And, he killed her."

"Yes." The one word was filled with a wealth of pain. I tightened my arms around him.

After a few seconds of silence, he continued, "Apparently, he'd been biding his time, working here until I came into the full inheritance on my thirtieth birthday. I'm not sure if he was going to sue us for his share or kill us." He barked out a humorless chuckle. "The irony is, if I'd known about him, I'd have gladly given him his share. I would love to have had a brother."

My heart broke just a little more for him. He was a good man. He didn't deserve all that had happened. "I guess Eleanor wasn't of the same mindset."

His chin rubbed my hair as he shook his head. "No, she already resented my inheriting before her. I tried to give her everything, including the bed and breakfast she wanted, but nothing ever made her happy."

"Poor Holt," I whispered. "I suspected him for a short while. They fought before her death."

"They fought all the time. But he would never have hurt her."

When Eleanor led me to their floor, she must have been trying to direct me to Troy. And the argument Jean had mentioned could have been about anything, maybe his affairs. "I wonder if we'll ever find where Jean hid Eleanor's necklace."

He gave a sad smile. "As it turns out, the police found it. She had a box of chocolate-covered cherries in her dresser drawer. The necklace was hidden in the bottom of the box." A note of affection colored his tone. He must miss her terribly. "The police are going to release it to me after they've completed the investigation."

I sat up away from him and looked into his face. "I am so sorry. For all you've been through. All you've lost. I wish I could do something to help."

"You can." His voice was hushed. He took both my hands in his. "Stay."

"I—do what?"

"Stay with me, Camille. The thought of you leaving tears me apart. I know we haven't known one another long, and you probably think I'm an asshole, but I promise, I'm not a bad guy, and I'd like to prove that to you."

My heart stilled, then beat entirely too fast. "You would?"

"Yeah. I would. I'm falling for you. I have never felt this way about another woman. Never met anyone like you. I wish you would stick around. I'd like to see where this thing between us might lead."

The faint note of pleading in his tone did me in.

I didn't have to think about it. I could write just as

well here. I didn't know if he meant *live* with him, but it was too soon for that. I'd have to find a place of my own. Move my things from Florida. But right now, all I wanted was to be with him. We could figure out the logistics later.

"Yes."

He waited, seeming to barely breathe. Then, his eyes narrowed. "Yes? You'll stay?"

I nodded happily. "I will. Yes."

"Thank God." He cupped my head in his hands and pressed his mouth to mine.

This time, I had no doubt the kiss meant something.

A word about the author...

Alicia Dean began writing stories as a child. At age 10, she wrote her first ever romance (featuring a hero who looked just like Elvis Presley, and who shared the name of Elvis' character in the movie, Tickle Me), and she still has the tattered, pencil-written copy. Alicia is from Moore, Oklahoma and now lives in Edmond. She has three grown children and a huge network of supportive friends and family. She writes mostly contemporary suspense and paranormal, but has also written in other genres, including a few vintage historicals.

Other than reading and writing, her passions are Elvis Presley (she almost always works in a mention of him into her stories), the MLB and NFL, and watching (and rewatching) her favorite televisions shows like Dexter, Justified, Ozark, The Office, I Love Lucy, Friends, and Justified. Some of her favorite authors are Michael Connelly, Dennis Lehane, Stephen King, Lee Child, Lisa Gardner, Ridley Pearson, Joseph Finder, and Jonathan Kellerman…to name a few.

Find Alicia here:
Website: http://aliciadean.com/
Facebook:
https://www.facebook.com/AuthorAliciaDean/
Twitter: @Alicia_Dean_
BookBub:
https://www.bookbub.com/profile/alicia-dean

Thank you for purchasing
this publication of The Wild Rose Press, Inc.

For questions or more information
contact us at
info@thewildrosepress.com.

The Wild Rose Press, Inc.
www.thewildrosepress.com